Trestle Rat

The Story of Al
By D.M. Williams

Table of Contents

The Lure of the South

The Southern language is as diverse alone as the many languages of the world. I never tire of listening to the people around me as I go about my day. It's pleasantly difficult to find two people with the exact same dialect. Many will agree this is the allure of the language indeed, with a sex appeal of its own. My personal favorite is the Deep South rhythmic drawl, the sexy accent that can easily hold its own besides the romantic French Gallo. The ear tingling high pitch twang rarely goes un-noticed much like the beautiful woman you never expect to see it hurling from when you look suddenly in its direction. Then there's the melodic Cajun rhythms of creole that make your heart dance to its fast pace poetic tempo. And let's be real, the south wouldn't be genuine without the flavorful dramatic grammar that each of us seems to perfect to our own liking literally changing mundane words into lavish works of art to sculpt our beautiful way of communicating. I believe the southern dialect has a romance of its own far beyond comparison. I have tried to depict only a few of these tantalizing dialects in my works to celebrate what I believe is The Lure of the South. Y'all enjoy now!

1

THE ACCIDENT

Early Friday morning after Thanksgiving, Alan headed out with his family to Jacksonville, Florida. He had business there concerning a new project scheduled to begin the first of the year. Rob had asked him to call when they got on the road, but he knows Rob has the night shift with the quadruplets, so he waited until later that morning to give him a call. They stopped for breakfast in Alabama. He called just before getting back on the road around 10:30. "I didn't call soon'r cause I didn't wanna wake ya up. I know yur runnin graveyard."

"Thanks. But I'm getting' used to that. Where're you guys?" Barlow asked.

"Halfway through Alabama. We'll be there by late eve'nin'," Alan told him.

"You could've been there soon'r if you had taken da plane," Rob scolded. He had told him when he made him partner that the plane was at his avail any time he needed it.

"I could also be there soon'r if you let me load up and get outta h're too," Alan argued. "Besides, I told you I like ta drive."

"I know, Buddy. Handle ya business."

Alan arrived in Jacksonville around 8pm much like he planned. His meeting with Mr. Miller was scheduled for 9am Saturday morning. He had no choice but to call Rob possibly waking him. Both men had agreed to be at the meeting. Alan called traditionally first to make certain Rob was up. Then he switched to a video call.

Once his meeting with Mr. Miller ended and all work was done, Alan spent the rest of the day enjoying the city with his family. They started at the zoo. AJ has developed an insatiable love for animals since he was introduced to The Grove. The zoo was interesting enough but not nearly as intriguing as the wild cats at the Catty Shack Ranch. AJ was having a ball admiring the big cats. His first time ever seeing a fully grown lion left him in awe. "Wow Dad!" he said, "Look at his mane. He's huge."

"Yeah, you wouldn't wanna meet him in da jungle *any time* of day," Alan warned.

"I wouldn't wanna meet any of 'em," Michelle added. As excited as AJ was, it was a little too close for comfort for Michelle.

"Come on, Mic. You gotta admit. They're beautiful."

"Un hun," she agreed, "but they'd look even more beautiful if we w're farther away from 'em." Alan thought that was funny. He chuckled.

"Mom. Stop being a baby," AJ told her, "they're locked up. They can't get to us."

"Un hun, but if you call me a baby one more time, I'm gon' throw ya lit'le butt ov'r da fence to 'em. We'll see who da baby is then," Michelle told AJ. On occasion she had to remind him who the parent is.

Alan figured he'd better play interference before things got ugly. He thought Christmas would get them back in a jolly mood. He decided a little Christmas shopping would clear Mic's mind of the wild cats. So, they found their way over to St. Johns Town Center where they ended their visit after shopping and an early dinner before heading back to Mississippi. "Are you sure you don't need to rest first? You've been going nonstop since early this morning."

"Thanks for da concern." He kissed his wife. "But I'm good."

"Thanks for inviting us along," Michelle replied, "I've missed our road trips. That reminds me. When are we takin' da motor home out?"

"You know what?" Alan asked. "We should make plans for that soon. I'll talk to Rob about it when we get home. I'd like us all to go together. Yor's and AJ's suggestions are always first priority though."

"I'm gonna be thinkin' about it."

A little over three hours into the ride, Alan stopped at the pump for a top-off so he could have a steady travel through most of the evening. AJ settled into the ride with his snacks and video games. Michelle enjoyed a snuggle like she used to always do when they accompanied him on his trips. Then Alan enjoyed the drive having his family with him.

Just at the hint of dusk, he noticed a vehicle coming up close behind him at a ridiculously fast speed. There was also a vehicle meeting him from the opposite direction. The car behind him wasn't slowing. Alan had no time to react. It zoomed past him without breaking. The vehicle approaching from the opposite side swerved to keep from hitting the car head on. It managed somehow to miss the car. But it spun out of control and was headed straight for Alan. His immediate prayer is that he would be able to save his family. There was no missing the vehicle, so he turned so that his side would absorb the most impact from the collision. Upon impact the truck flipped a full cartwheel over the car before setting back up on all four wheels. The other vehicle left the road to hit a tree.

Michelle miraculously walked away from the crash with a fractured collarbone and whiplash. AJ seated closer to Alan on the driver side of the truck suffered a broken arm and complained of neck and chest pain also. Alan was knocked unconscious and taken away immediately because of his serious injuries. When Michelle regained her composure, she called Barlow to let him know what happened.

#

Barlow was helping Chasidy with a diaper change when his phone rang. "Its Mic." He told Chasidy after glancing at his phone.

"Go ahead, I got this," She told him. Mic was crying hysterically. Chasidy could hear her through the phone. Rob tried to calm her.

"Mic, I can't understand you. Calm down Honey and tell me what's hap'ning." She calmed herself briefly then started up again, no better than she was before. But he could hear AJ yelling to him.

"Uncle Rob, we w're in an accident! Dad's hurt bad!"

Barlow tried to get Michelle calm again. "Mic, where are you?"

"I don't know. I was asleep. I don't know," she spoke in confusion.

"Ask da nurse..." he began to say, but then OnStar contacted him. "Mic. OnStar is on da line. Let me call you right back." When he hung up from OnStar, he looked at Chasidy. It was a rhetorical question when he asked, "You up for trav'ling?" He wasn't her and the babies there alone, not knowing how long he would be away.

"What hap'ened?" she asked in return.

"They had an accident. Al's hurt bad." Then he called Sam to make ready for the trip. "Have da plane fueled. Get us as close as you can ta Lansing, Georgia."

"All of Us?" Sam asked.

"Plus one," Chasidy added, "I'll need help with da babies while you tend to yor family. I'll see if Caitlin can take some time off."

"Thank you," he said sincerely.

Chasidy had her on the phone even before Rob hung up from Sam. "We have an emergency. I need you to go to Georgia with me. Can you take a few days?"

Barlow told her, "If they won't let you off, you can quit and come work for me."

She could tell he sounded upset. Almost like when her mom was missing. "It's fine," Caitlin told them, "I don't miss many days. I'm sure its ok."

"They're getting' da plane ready. We'll pick you up in" she looked at Rob.

"Thirty minutes," he spoke answering her unasked question.

"Thirty minutes," she told Caitlin.

"You got that Sam?" Rob asked.

"Got it Sir."

Once loaded in the Bentley, Sam informed Barlow, "Lansing is just outside of Savannah, we'll land there. The hospital is less than twenty minutes away."

"Lodging?"

"Savannah-Hilton. Three rooms. Two adjoining."

"Thank ya Sam."

"At yor pleasure, Sir."

Barlow sat up front with Sam after they picked up Caitlin to allow her to sit with her mom. She took full advantage of playing with the babies. "They've gotten cuter since Thanksgiving," she told her mom.

Chasidy smiled. But even chatter about the babies couldn't keep her from worrying about Mic and Al. She had to call to see if she had calmed down. AJ answered the phone. "Sweetheart, how are you doing?" Barlow gestured for her to put him on speaker.

"I'm hurtin' Aunt Chasidy. Everywhere. My head, my back. My chest hurts really. They gave me some medicine. They say it's too soon to get more."

"I know it hurts, but da meds will kick in shortly."

"I hope so."

"Hang in there, Sweetheart. We're coman. Where's yor mom?"

"They had to make 'er sleep. She wouldn't calm down. They said somethin' about her heart. I don't know what that was though."

"AJ," Barlow interrupted, "Whatda you know about yor dad?"

"Nothin'. I'm scared, Uncle Rob. They told my mom somethin' about 'im and then they had to give 'er da medicine. She didn't get a chance to tell me. And they don't talk to kids h're."

"You lis'en ta Aunt Chasidy, Little Guy. Hang in there. When that medicine kicks in, you'll be able to rest. We're on our way," Rob told him. Then he called the hospital to find out what was going on with Alan and Michelle. The nurse at the nurse's station was reciting hospital rules to him about not being able to give out patient information over the phone.

The nurse who was just in the room with AJ when he was on the phone walked up to the desk in the middle of the down-spiraling conversation. "I'll take that." The nurse gladly handed her the phone. "Uncle Rob?' she asked him.

"Yes Robert Barlow. I'm tryin' ta find out how Alan and Michelle Ferguson are doing."

"I can help you with that. I was just in the room when you and your wife were talking to your nephew."

"Thank you," he said relieved. "He said she had to be sedated. Is Al ok?"

"Mr. Barlow. Let me first say, that Mr. Ferguson is still alive. That being said, the reason we had to sedate his wife is because during the operation, he coded. It took the doctors so long to bring him back, we thought we had lost him. We didn't tell Mrs. Ferguson all of that. We didn't have to. Once she heard the code blue, she became hysterical. That's why we had to calm her down. Quite naturally we didn't share any of that info with your nephew."

"Thank you Nurse ...?"

"Tammy."

"Nurse Tammy. We're own our way there from Mississippi. We should be there in about two hours. I'll look you up when I get there."

"My shift will be ending just about that time, but I'll stick around to give you an update. Plus, I'm the only familiar face your nephew knows right now until his mom wakes up. I'll sit with him until you get here."

"You don't know how much we appreciate that. Thank you." Before he hung up he remembered Michelle's heart condition. "Nurse Tammy, is da doctor aware of Mic's heart condition?"

"Yes, she was unconscious when she arrived, but that sharp nephew of yours made sure we knew before we gave her any medications."

"My little man," Barlow spoke proudly. "See ya in two hours."

#

Once they settled at the hotel, Rob made haste to leave for the hospital. "I'll call you with an update." he said to Chasidy.

"You won't have to. I'm going with you," she replied.

"What about da babies?" He questioned.

"Caitlin can handle them for an hour. I promise I'll come back afta' that." She searched his eyes for compassion. "I won't get any rest until I look into Mic's face and give AJ a hug. He's gotta be scared, Rob. Don't you dare keep me away from them. Not when they need me."

He turned for a quick confirmation from Caitlin. "Go. I got this."

#

By now, hospital scenes were becoming second nature to Barlow. Like a second home of sorts. Nurse Tammy was indeed sitting with AJ when they entered the room. He was so glad to see familiar faces that he started crying. "Uncle Rob, Aunt Chasidy!" He yelled. "I'm so scared. I haven't seen my dad since I've been h're and mom is still sleepin'. I don't know what to do?" he spoke non-stop.

"Don't worry about yor dad. They're takin' good care-a him. You just concentrate on feelin' bett'r. I'm gonna talk ta da nurse, see what I can find out about yor dad, ok?"

"Ok. Uncle Rob."

Rob gave him a comforting hug and extended a gentle kiss on Michelle's forehead before leaving the room to speak to the nurse. Chasidy followed suit with her own kiss to the forehead before she climbed into bed with AJ holding him in her arms. "We're h're now. You try to get some rest."

#

"Thankyou again for stayin' with 'im," Barlow said.

"No need to thank me. I couldn't leave 'im. He refused to go to sleep as long as his mother was out. Maybe now he'll get some rest."

"That's my little man," Barlow said proudly. "What can you tell me about Al?"

#

By the time AJ was fully asleep, Michelle had awakened. "Shh," Chasidy told her easing out of bed. "He just went to sleep."

"How long have you been h're?" Michelle asked.

"Only about twenty minutes."

"Da babies?"

"Caitlin has them. She's h're with us."

"Rob?"

"He's checkan' on Alan."

Michelle sat up a little. "I'm a terrible mom. I just left him hangin' ta deal with this all by 'imself. I was so scared, Chasidy. I think I lost 'im. I think Al is gone."

"I know. Da nurse explained. But you didn't lose 'im. He's still with us." Chasidy consoled, giving her a hug. Chasidy tried to lighten things up a little. "Girl, we just can't stay away from these hospitals can we? Every time we go to a new city, we have to try one out."

Michelle tried to laugh. "That would've been a lot funnier if Al was h're to hear it too." She burst into tears again. "When is Rob comin' back? I need to know how Al's doin'."

"I'm right h're." He heard her as he opened the door. "I was just getting' da full story from nurse Tammy. First of all, Al is alive. He's in a coma though. When da truck flipped, he hit his head a few times."

"Da truck flipped?" Michelle asked.

"Yes, a couple of times b'fore settin' back up on da tires." B'cause of that he's pretty traumatized."

"But how is he hurt so badly and AJ and I ...?"

"Well, a'cordin' to a witness, when Al saw that y'all w're gonna be hit head-on, he turned so that his side would get da biggest impact. If he hadn't done that, none of you would've come outta this alive. A'cordin' to da highway patrolman."

"What hap'ened to da person who hit us?" Michelle asked. "I'll bet they w're drunk."

"No. It wasn't her fault. She was hurt really badly also. She had her two-year-old son in da car with 'er. It's a modern-day God-given miracle that he wasn't hurt. Nurse Tammy said it's a miracle they're all even alive after hittin' Alan and a tree."

"Then what caused da accident?" Chasidy asked.

"An idiot speedin' and passin' when there was no clear right of way. He was too close to Alan and da approachin' car. He nev'r stopped."

"It was a hit and run?" Chasidy asked.

"Yeah," Barlow answered, "except he didn't get hit."

"And now my husband's fightin' for his life and me and my son are layin' in hospital beds."

"Well, let's concentrate on da positive," Barlow encourage. "Yur all still alive."

Chasidy looked at her phone. She promised to only be gone for an hour. It would take twenty minutes to get back to the hotel. Barlow noticed her checking the time. "Are you ready for Sam?"

She reluctantly nodded yes. She didn't want to leave her friend so soon. But she didn't have a choice. She said to Michelle. "I wish I could stay. I promised Caitlin I'd be back in an hour. I just had to see you and AJ fa myself. I'm glad you woke up b'fore I had to leave." She gave her another hug. "Be proud of that son of yors. Nurse Tammy said he really did you a solid."

"I am proud of 'im," she said in her weakened voice, "he's so much like his dad. Especially in times like this."

"Get betta, sistar. I'll try to get back t'morrow."

"I'm gonna walk 'er to da car. I'll be back," Barlow assured Michelle.

"Is there any way I can peek at Alan b'fore I go?" she asked once they were in the hallway.

"You could." Barlow said not so confidently. "He's in ICU. But, will you trust me that you don't wanna do that just yet," he told her as they entered the elevator.

Looking away in tears, she nodded her head sadly. He turned her face back towards him with his finger. "He's gonna be alright. It's just that he's an Alan we're not used to seein'. I don't want you to see 'im like that."

"Lis'en at you," she said with a half-smile, "I should be encouragin' you. But you sound like you truly b'lieve that."

"I do." Ushering her into the car, he said, "kiss da babies for me."

2

LOVE AT FIRST SIGHT

hile in the coma however, Alan began to see his life rehearse before him from the childhood he had reminisced in his mind a little more than often. Thoughts of how he left the orphanage as a boy rolled around in his head. It kept his mind busy with memories both happy and sad. He was still unable to recapture any memories of his parents. No matter how hard he tried. When he heard the comforting voice of his best friend, he immediately remembered his lonely journey to Amory, Mississippi. It was there he met his never-imagined lifelong friend, Robert Barlow. He smiled in his mind at the memory of their unique love-at-first-sight meeting.

§

"Okay Lil' Ferguson, time to get up," the attendant at the Chiricahua Children's Home told him. "It's

MEET ME DAY, r'member? We may find you some parents b'fore da day's ov'r," she said excitedly. She was certainly more excited than Alan was. He wasn't interested in just any family. He was only interested in his family. His real family. At barely six years old, that was already a definite state of mind for him. His heart's desire even, so-to-speak.

Another attendant came in with some freshly ironed clothes. "Look h're Alan. Aren't these nice?" she asked him. Alan didn't answer her. "Hey Cutie, don't you hear me?"

"Yes," he answered.

"Yes?" She said with a slightly raised voice. "So, why ain't you talkin' this mornin'? Cat got yo tongue?"

"No," he answered, "I got my own tongue." Both attendants laughed at the six-year old's adorable reply.

"Are you excited about taday?" the first attendant asked.

"No." Alan answered.

"You should be! Don't you want nice parents to live with in a nice home of ya own? Handsome lil' guy like you. That won't take long at all. Shoot. I've a mind to take you myself."

"I 'on't know," he answered. But then added, "Will they be my real parents?"

"If they decide to adopt ya," she answered.

"What's that?" he asked.

"Adopt? That means they can ask da state of Miss'sippi to allow them to be yor parents. Then you'll be rightfully their son," the attendant explained.

"Oh," Alan said. Ever since he was old enough to think, all he thought about what his mom and dad were like. Where they were. And why he wasn't with them. It didn't sound to him like the people who would adopt him would be his real parents. He didn't want to go with strangers. *'Adopt ain't family. Adopt is strangers. Family is family.'* He thought. "I 'on't want no adopt," he said. "I want my mom and dad."

The attendant stared at him compassionately. "I don't know what hap'ened to yor mom and pop, but I'm sure they would come for ya if they could." She gave him a little comfort hug. "Well, you might change yor lil' mine if you meet some folks you like."

When the big people started arriving, he tried to stay hidden away from them as much as possible. If anyone was clever enough to find him, he just stayed quiet like he couldn't talk and didn't understand what they were saying. That worked out well for him for the next three years. On his ninth birthday, he promised himself that when he became ten, he would ditch the children's home and go find his real family.

Chiricahua didn't know much about him other than he was the lone survivor of an automobile accident that caused his parents' death. He didn't remember the accident or his parents. The doctors called his type of amnesia Dissociative. For some unexplained reason, they had difficulty finding his birth records. When that happens, the Home appointed the day they arrived at the facility as their birthday. This had been the case with Alan. One year later before the next MEET ME DAY, he packed a sack of snacks he had been saving up, along with a few pieces of clothing and a winter jacket. Then he left Chiricahua Children's Home at 12:15 am after everyone else had fallen asleep.

Looking straight ahead imagining the family he would one day find, he never looked back and never regretted leaving. He ran as fast as his little legs could carry him, gathering trinkets along the way that caught his interest. Putting them away in his bag; he held on to them because he liked putting things together. He passed time doing that whenever he'd stop to rest. His only other stops were to nap and have a bite to eat in nooks and crannies hidden away from the world. It wasn't until his food supply ran out on him five days later about twenty miles away from Chiricahua, that he lingered in the small town of Amory hoping to find something to eat.

A nice couple took notice of him one day when they were out for an afternoon stroll around town. He was perched under a streetlamp by a nearby restaurant watching the patrons enjoy their meals. The couple could see he was hungry. The woman approached him while her husband went on to order their food. "Hello young man. My husband is or'derin' lunch. Would you care to join us?" Alan stood to run away, but the woman stopped him. "Please don't run! We just wanna get you somethin' ta eat. You are hungry, aren't ya?" she asked him politely.

Alan tried to size the woman up. He looked at her shyly for just a few minutes. She had a pretty smile and a nice voice. And she smelled good too. He decided she was okay to talk to. Then he asked, "Which one's yor husband?" directing his attention now to the people standing in line at the counter of the small café.

"He's da one wearing da red cap," she answered. The man also looked alright enough to Alan. And he liked his red cap. He just wasn't sure about eating with strangers. He wondered if they were 'adopt' people.

The woman must have read his mind. She kneeled closer to him and asked him, "What's yor name, Sweetie?"

"Alan," he answered.

"Well, Alan, my name is Kelly. Kelly Marshall. My husband's name is Stan. We really would love for you to join us. But you need to make up yor mind. He's almost ready to order," she persuaded.

Alan thought a minute longer. "Well, alright," he agreed reluctantly, even though he hadn't eaten in over a day and his stomach was growling at him. They walked over to a vacant table and waited for Mr. Marshall to come with the food. Alan could practically taste the burger when he saw Mr. Marshall approaching the table with the tray. He sat Alan's meal down in front of him right off. Alan lit in first thing on the fries. He was so hungry; he didn't bother with the ketchup.

They let him eat his fill before asking about his situation. Not really knowing how to approach the subject, Mrs. Marshall started with an introduction. "Stan, this handsome little guy is Alan. Alan, this handsome big guy is my husband Stanley. But everybody calls him Stan." Alan giggled at her introduction.

"Pleased to meet ya Alan," Mr. Marshall said.

Alan raised his head from eating to look at Mr. Marshall. "Nice to meet you Sir. Thank you fa da food," he said with a jaw full.

"What's a lit'le tyke like you doing out here in this big ol' world all by yorself? Where're yor folks?" he asked Alan.

Alan didn't want to answer that question. He didn't want them to take him back to the children's home. He hadn't found his family yet. And he didn't know if they were 'adopt' people or not. So, he played it as safe as he knew how. He stopped eating his lunch and began to wrap it up in the wrapper it came in. "Thanks again for da food. I have to go now."

"Don't leave," Mrs. Marshall said. "Stan didn't mean to pry. We're just concerned about you."

"I have to go see about my mom. She's home sick."

They had a feeling he wasn't being truthful and just trying to get away from them. Mr. Marshall offered his help. "Sit and finish eatin' yor food, Son. I can buy somethin' for yor mom if you'd like."

"It's alright," Alan said, "we can share mine."

"Well at least let us drop ya off," he offered.

Alan didn't want them to become suspicious, so he agreed. He picked the prettiest house he saw three blocks away and said, "Right h're. You can drop me h're."

"This is yor home?" Mrs. Marshall asked. But Alan rushed out of the car without answering. He stood waving goodbye until they drove away before starting towards the house. The Marshalls knew this wasn't his home. They knew the people who lived there. It was a little old couple who had been there for years and never had children. But what could they do?

Alan had become an expert by now at finding nesting places. As soon as the Marshalls were out of site, he darted behind the house and over to the next ally to look for a place to bed down for the night. He didn't know how far he had traveled but he knew it took him a long time to get here. He decided he would hang here a few days to rest his legs before moving on.

The Marshalls would run into him ever-so-often, always offering to buy him a bite to eat. He always reluctantly accepted. With each offer of a meal also came an offer to come live with them. This went on for over a month. He kept coming up with cute lies and crafty excuses why he couldn't leave his sick mother.

One day just towards the end of summer, Mrs. Marshall laid it all out on the table for him. "Alright lit'le guy. Enough is enough. We know yur da child who was missing from Chiricahua. We don't care about that. You don't have to worry about going back there," she told him. "Da place burned down da night you went missing. We have wondered how you made it this far by yorself, though."

Mr. Marshall added, "Yeah, yur a brave lit'le guy. And you can trust us. We care about you. We really want you to come live with us. Da streets are no place for a child. Even one as brave as you are."

Even though he was only ten, Alan had survivor etched in him. Fall was close approaching and winter would set in quickly thereafter. He decided if nothing else, he would spend the cold months with them indoors and start his journey again in the spring. But. He wasn't giving up on finding his family. "Well, if yur sure I won't be no both'r," he said.

"We're perfectly sure," Mrs. Marshall said.

Life was good for Alan with the Marshalls. They treated him well, took care of him, bought things for him, took him to movies and parks and other things he didn't know families do. When the first spring came much sooner than Alan thought it should have, he decided he would wait until the next one to move on. He liked the Marshalls a lot. But, as much as he enjoyed being with them, they weren't his family. And the itch to find his own family was beginning to rise again. He tried to ignore it because the Marshalls had been so good to him. He even tried to convince himself that they could be some of his family. He realized he didn't look like most black folks he had seen. But, he had to admit, he didn't look like them either, white folks. The more he thought about it, the more the urge grew for him to move on. *'There has to be somebody out there who looks like me.'* He thought.

#

One summer day, out of boredom, he went for a walk to the other side of Amory to see the rest of the small town he had nestled in. He had been here two years now and still didn't know much about it. He ran across a neat little pond, so he made a fishing pole with some of his trinkets he carried around in his pocket. He hadn't come prepared to fish so when he caught one, he laid it on a pile of grass and continued fishing. The big black cat that liked to hang around the pond decided he would invite himself to Alan's lunch. He quietly snatched up the fish while Alan was facing the pond.

Alan turned around just in time to see him run off. The big cat scrambled up a nearby tree determined to keep his free lunch. Alan was determined to get it back. He climbed up the tree behind the cat. That old cat sat at the edge of a branch watching Alan trying his darndest to get to him. When Alan thought he was close enough, he reached for the cat, but lost his balance and fell. The cat watched Alan hit the ground, then slowly scrambled off with his fish.

"Son of Sam!" Alan yelled at the cat as he got up rubbing his head. "If I catch you round h're again, da fish'll be eatin' you!" Then he heard laughter behind him and turned to see who it was.

"You alright!" the boy asked still laughing. "You hit da ground pretty hard."

"I'm fine," Alan told him. "But that cat won't be if he shows his face 'round h're again."

"Sounds like yur gonna have a fight on yor hands. Ol' Smokey's round h're all da time," the boy said. "My name's Rob. What's yors?"

"Alan," he replied.

"Alan, you sure yur alright? You fell from pretty high up."

"Yeah, I'm sure. I'm tough enough," Alan told him.

"I nev'r seen you round h're b'fore. You just move h're?" Rob asked him.

"Not exactly," Alan answered.

"Well... what exactly?" Rob probed.

"Mor' like passin' through. I'm lookin' for my folks." Alan explained.

"Whatta their names? Maybe I can help ya look. I know a lotta folks round h're."

Alan leaned his head slightly to one side. He didn't really want to say, but he had no choice. I 'on't know their names," he said disappointedly.

"Well, where're you from? Maybe you could start there," Rob tried to help.

"I ain't from nowhere," Alan answered.

"Everybody's from somewhere," Rod argued.

"Not everybody. And da nowhere I'm from don't know nothin' 'bout me. So, I have to find out for ma' self."

"Well, I'll still help ya if ya want me to." They hung out by the pond the rest of the day. Rob was fascinated with his handmade fishing pole. Alan helped him make one for himself. He even shared his beef jerky with him for bait. "If you don't have no folks, who taught you how to make a fishin' pole like this?"

"Nobody," Alan said. "Puttin' things t'gether is just in my head." Rob understood that. There was stuff rolling around in his head also that no one taught him.

Rob caught a fish bigger than the one Ol' Smokey stole from Alan. "This is a nice one," he said grinning. "Why 'on't you come have dinn'r with us? Ma Ethel'll fry him up real nice."

"Naw, I don't wanna be no both'r." Alan said sadly.

"If you w're a both'r, I wouldn't have asked ya," Rob explained.

"Thanks, but I gotta go." Alan picked up his make-shift pole and started slowly walking away. A strange feeling came over him as he walked. He didn't understand it. But. He didn't want to leave.

Rob, experiencing his own unexplainable feelings, yelled to him, "Nowhere can't be that far from h're. I could walk ya halfway aft'r we eat."

It would be dark soon and Alan hadn't found him a place to perch for the night. It wasn't his intention to stay away from the Marshalls when he left their house today. They're probably worried sick about him by now. The more he walked away, the more something tugged at him to go back. He turned around to see Rob standing there watching him. "You waitin' for me?" he asked him.

"Yeah," Rob answered. "You comin'?"

Something inside him was elated. He really wanted to stay anyway. "Well, okay," Alan agreed. "But I can't stay long."

#

Ethel was in the kitchen as usual. She was just about to start dinner because she made it home late from her rounds in the community checking up on the elderly. "Ma Ethel, look what we got!" Rob entered the house calling to Ethel.

"First off, who's we?" she asked looking at the huge fish Rob was holding up. "That's a nice dinn'r for this eve'nin'. Good thing I haven't started yet. Put 'im in da sink."

"We, is my new friend…" Rob started to introduce Alan, but Alan wasn't there. He stepped back out onto the porch to get him. But he wasn't there either. When he found him, he was sitting on the steps at the front of the house. He had tried again to leave, but that was as far as he got. "You got one more try," Rob told him.

"What's that mean?" Alan asked.

"You w're gonna leave, w'ren't ya?" Rob read his mind.

"No," Alan lied. Rob just stared at him. "Yeah," he then confessed.

"Why you in such a hurry to go back to nowhere?" This time Alan did the staring. "I heard Ma Ethel say one time that da third time's a charm. Maybe you'll make it da next time." Rob started into the house. "Yur still welcome ta dinn'r."

Ethel was thrilled to meet him. But Alan was quiet. "I thought I knew most of da young'uns round h're," she said to Alan. "You must be with that new family that moved ov'r on Cary St. I didn't hear tell-a them with children though," she babbled on.

"Yes Mam," Alan said. Rob wondered why he was lying. He didn't talk much during dinner. He was wondering what the Marshalls were thinking at the moment. He hoped they weren't worrying too much.

After dinner, Rob walked Alan halfway to nowhere which ended up being near the old railroad trestle.

Alan told him he could make it the rest of the way alone. But instead, he found a soft spot under the trestle to bed down for the night. He wanted to go back. But he was afraid they wouldn't let him come back. He felt bad that he was making them worry about him. He had to fix that. They were good people. But for some reason, this place had a special feel to it, even if he didn't have a home here. He rose early the next morning to make his way back to the other side of Amory to let the Marshalls know he was alright. And to tell them the time had come for him to leave.

#

Mrs. Marshall was in tears when Alan walked through the door. He was dirty from sleeping on the ground under the trestle, but she didn't care about that. She hugged him and kissed him like her prodigal son had returned home. "We were worried sick about you," she told him. "Where were you? What happened to you?"

"I know. I'm fine. I'm sorry," Alan apologized sincerely. "That's why I came back." When Mr. Marshall entered the room, Alan was met with the same greeting from him. After seeing them carry on so over him, he didn't have the heart to leave them again so soon.

"Don't ever scare us like that again!" Mrs. Marshall told him.

"I won't. I promise."

For nearly a week Alan moped around the house in quiet thought. He did extra chores to keep his hands busy and went to bed early sometimes to collect his thoughts.

Kelly and Stan knew something was bothering him. He just hadn't been the same since he had gotten back. It was as if, he left their Alan along the road somewhere. They wanted him back. "Stan. I think we need to talk to Alan, try to find out what happened to 'im while he was away." Kelly told her husband one morning just before breakfast.

"You noticed it too, huh? I didn't mention it because I didn't wanna upset you." Stan explained.

"Has he said anything at all to you?"

"No. Nothing." When he got up that morning, they asked him to join them in the living room.

"Did I do somethin' wrong?" he asked.

"The way you've been working around here," Stan said. "I have to read the newspaper twice just to have something to do." Alan smiled. "Sit down with us a minute. Kelly and I wanna talk to ya."

"Alan, we noticed you haven't been da same since you got back. Are you alright?"

"Yes Mam."

"Well, did something happen to ya son? You're just not ya'self."

Alan didn't know how to explain it. And he didn't know how to tell them that he needed to leave. So, he answered their question. "Well. I fell outta a tree and hit my head."

"What!" Mrs. Marshall yelped. "Why didn't you say something? You could have a concussion."

But Mr. Marshall wanted to hear the whole story. "Let's let 'im finish, Dear. How'd you come to fall?"

"I was tryin' to get my fish back?"

"Your fish?" he asked.

"Yeah," Alan said, speaking in bits and pieces, trying to prolong the news they didn't want to hear. "I caught 'im while I was fishin'. A cat stole 'im from me." Mr. Marshall chuckled at that. But he didn't interrupt him. "He climbed up a tree and I climbed up aft'r 'im. That's when I fell."

"Is that why you didn't make it home that day?" Mrs. Marshall asked. "And why you were so dirty?"

Alan was tempted to say yes. But he couldn't lie to them. Especially since he was about to break their hearts. "No Mam." A quietness formed in the room. His eyes began to fill with tears. He couldn't bear to look at them.

"Alan," Mrs. Marshall urged, "what are you not telling us?"

Alan burst into full blown tears. He didn't know how to tell them about the boy. How he beckons for him. How he had to get back to him. He didn't know of an easy way to do it, so he just blurted it out. "I can't stay," he said to them. "I came back because I didn't want you worryin' 'bout me."

"Whatta you mean, Son?" Mr. Marshall asked. "Why can't ya stay?"

Alan hated hurting them. But he didn't know what else to do. Something was pulling him back to the boy across town. "That's what I mean," he paused. "I'm not really yor son," he said with tears in his eyes.

Mrs. Marshall had feared this day from the time they convinced him to come live with them. Her initial hope was that if they loved him enough, he would want to stay. She wanted to hear the entire story. She wanted to know what happened that day to cause him to want to leave them. However, she had heard as much as she could handle at the moment. She needed time to for that to soak in. "Have you washed up yet?"

"No Mam."

"Why don't you go do that," she said. "Breakfast will be ready when you come down. You can finish telling us about it then." Alan started slowly up the stairs. "Alan," she called after him.

"Mam?" he answered.

"You could be our son, if ya wanted to be." She said. Alan didn't respond to that.

The words tossed around in his head over and over. *'They are adopt people,'* he thought. But realizes now that adopt people aren't so bad after all. Part of him wanted to stay and become their son. But then there was the boy. If he was going to do this, it had to be today; before he lost his nerve. The Marshalls were only supposed to be temporary.

He came back down with a small sack packed. He left it at the bottom of the stairs before entering the kitchen. "Can I take these?" he asked them.

"When you said you couldn't stay, we didn't know you meant you were leaving today. Sit down and talk to us Alan," Mr. Marshall insisted. "We need to understand what's going on."

"Eat your breakfast first," Mrs. Marshall ordered. "If you're gonna leave us, I wanna know that your belly is full b'fore you do."

As Alan ate, he explained that for as long as he can remember, the only wish he's had is to find his people. Someone who is related to him. His own parents even. Everyone else has family, why wouldn't he? "That's why I left da Children's Home in da first place. I gotta have family somewhere," he said.

"That's why you w're reluctant to come home with us?" Mr. Marshall asked.

"Yes Sir." Alan said.

"What hap'ened yes'erday ta make you wanna leave us now?" Mrs. Marshall asked.

"Nothin' special," Alan said. "I 'on't think. It's just that..."

"What?" she nudged.

"I met somebody. This person feels...." Alan paused from eating his breakfast. "That place.... feels.... right."

"Do you think they might be your family?" she asked.

"No. I 'on't know. I 'on't think so," he answered confused. "But I really wanted to stay."

"Why don't you stay here and let us meet these people first. Make sure they're good people," Mr. Marshall pleaded.

"He is good people," Alan said hurriedly.

"He?" They both asked.

"Yeah. A boy, 'bout my age, I think." Alan paused again. "When I met 'im, I didn't wanna leave 'im. And now that I have, I have to go back." He spoke slowly and solemnly. "And... I 'on't think he wanted me to leave eith'r."

"But you're both children. Where will you stay?" they asked Alan. "Who will take care of you?"

"I can take care of ma'self," he said. "I'm tough enough."

"That's absurd son," Mr. Marshall protested. "I won't let you do this. Anything could hap'en to you."

Alan dropped his head. He didn't have all the answers they needed. He didn't have the answers he needed. He just knew he had to get back to Rob. "I love you guys too and I 'on't mean ta hurt you. You've been good to me. I 'on't have to take da bag if you 'on't want me to. But ... I am leavin'. Please don't be mad at me."

Mrs. Marshall hugged Alan, squeezing him as tight as she could before running into the living room crying. Mr. Marshall's eyes were in tears also. "Are you sure you wanna do this?"

"Yes sir. I am."

He sighed grievously. "We're not mad at you Son. We hope you find your family. You take whatev'r you need, as much of it as you need." He pulled out his wallet and handed him all the money he had in it. "Take this too. If you need anything, anything at all, come back to me to get it. You hear me, Son? You come back to me."

Alan picked up his small sack and left but not before giving Mr. Marshall a long hug also. "I'll be back to visit. I promise. I won't fa'get about you." When he reached the street, he ran full speed back to Rob, again, never looking back.

#

Rob was experiencing his own separation anxiety while Alan was away. Alan wouldn't let him walk all the way home with him the night he left. Now he was wishing he had. He could've visited him at his home. Now he just has to wait until he comes back. If he comes back. He remembered him saying he was just passing through looking for his folks. He was hoping that had changed. He really wanted to see him again.

As soon as Alan left his sack under the old railroad trestle, he rushed off with his fishing pole to the pond to find Rob. Rob wasn't there so he headed over to his house and waited for him to come out.

Rob was happy to see him. He had missed him. "Hey! Where you been. I looked for ya down by da pond."

"You sayin' you missed me?"

"No." Rob said quickly. "I'm sayin' I looked for ya down by da pond," he repeated. Then admitted, "Well, maybe a little."

"Sorry. I couldn't get away. But I'm h're now. What cha wanna do?"

Rob had his community chores to see about, but, since Alan was back, he decided to hang out with him instead. "Well, I see you have yor fishin' pole. We could go fishin' again."

"Great! That ol cat bett'r not be around," Alan griped.

"He'll be around there somewhere. We'll keep a look out for 'im. Besides, we can take a bucket with us this time." They fished and played around all day. Alan didn't mention about going back to nowhere. And Rob didn't ask him if he had to leave.

When they got to Rob's house that evening, they had five fish to clean up. When he took them in to Ethel to show them off, he got an ear full. "Ma Ethel, look!" He held up the bucket full of fish.

"Boy, I've been worried about you all day! Folks been callin' me askin' where you are? You nev'r made it to anybody's house taday. Now I see why," she scolded.

"Sorry Ma. I didn't mean to skip out on everybody. But Alan's back!" he said excitedly.

Ethel saw how his mood had improved from just the day before. He had been barely moving about all week. She couldn't even be upset with him after seeing the big smile on his face. "Well. It looks like you had fun." Then she acknowledged Alan. "Welcome back, Alan. Y'all go round back and clean 'em up." As they headed back out the door, she stopped them. "Alan."

"Mam?"

"You should come around more often. Robert really does work too much." She smiled as she spoke.

Alan showed up at Rob's doorstep every morning so that Rob wouldn't find out he had taken up lodgings under the trestle. Rob invited him to dinner every evening just like when they first met and walked him halfway to nowhere when the day was over. Alan wouldn't go to dinner every day. He was afraid Ethel would figure out he was homeless. He was careful to manage the money he was given by his temporary dad. He used it only when he didn't have dinner with Rob. They hung out all summer long becoming inseparable. Until, that is, school started in the fall.

#

When Rob made his first day in school, Alan was nowhere in sight. He looked for him all day, but never found him. By the time he made it home to Ethel, he was miserable. "Who stole yor joy?" Ethel asked. "You w're excited about da first day of school when you left h're this mornin." Rob didn't say anything. He sat down at the table and pulled out his books to start doing his homework. "Robert, did somethin' hap'en at school?"

"No," he said. "Somethin' didn't hap'en."

Ethel sat down at the table with him. "What didn't hap'en, Dear Heart?"

"I didn't find Alan. I looked for 'im all day. I nev'r saw 'im," Rob said, never looking up from his history book.

Alan was right in his fears about Ethel. She did have suspicions about him being homeless. She refused to believe her son hadn't figured it out yet. "Robert, you've spent da entire summ'r with Alan. What've you learned about 'im?"

"Not much," Rob answered.

"Where's he from?" Ethel asked.

"Nowhere," Rob answered.

"Who are his people?" Ethel asked.

"Nobody," he said.

Ethel sat there staring at Rob until he raised his head to look up at her. "Robert. You know why Alan wasn't at school, don't ya?"

"No mam, I don't," he said.

"Alan is homeless, Baby."

"He ain't homeless!" Rob replied with an elevated tone.

"Mind who you raise yor voice at boy," Ethel scolded. She was as firm as she was gentle when she needed to be. She needed to be quite often, raising a boy to become a man. And not just any boy. But the child of her deceased best friend, Roberta Barlow.

"Yes Mam. I'm sorry." Rob apologized.

Ethel knew her son was smarter than that. She knew Rob wasn't completely blind to Alan's situation. If anything, he was in denial. "You did know that. Didn't ya Robert?" she asked him once more.

"I kinda figured," he finally admitted. "But I could nev'r get 'im ta tell me. He nev'r took me to his house. Every time we got close to that old railroad trussell he'd say he could walk da rest-a da way by 'imself."

"Da trussell," Ethel repeated.

"Yes..." Rob started to speak, but then stopped in thought. "Do ya think that's where he is?" he asked Ethel.

"I think it's a good place to start lookin' for 'im. I'm sure he's probably hungry by now."

"Yes Mam!" Rob said excitedly. "I'll go get 'im."

#

Sure enough, there he was tucked away sleeping in a nook under the trestle. "You been sleep h're all day?" Rob spoke loudly to wake him. "How come you wasn't at school? And how come you didn't tell me you don't have nowhere to stay, and you live under this old trussell?" Rob yelled question after question at him.

"You want me to answer all dem questions at da same time or answer 'em one by one?" Alan yelled back.

"I thought we w're friends, Al. Why didn't you tell me you needed a place to stay?"

"Cause I have a place to stay," Alan told him.

"Winter's comin'. You can't stay h're all winter, you'll freeze." Rob spoke with compassion. Alan could tell he really cared about him.

"Well, Fall's gotta get h're first," Alan responded. "I'll be alright. I'm tough enough."

"Come on," Rob said.

"Where?" Alan asked.

"Where you think?" Rob asked in return. "Home. Ta eat. I'm hungry."

"Ma Ethel know?" Alan asked.

"Who ya think told me?" Rob answered with a question.

"Great. That's all I need."

Rob was concerned for Alan. He couldn't imagine him enjoying living under a railroad track. "You been livin' und'r that trussell all yor life?"

"No, just this summ'r."

"Where w're you b'fore then?"

"Stayin' with some folks on da oth'r side-a town." Alan finally shared.

"Inside a house?" Rob asked with a raised voice.

"Yeah, a big pretty house too," Alan added.

"What would make you leave a big pretty house ta live und'r a trussell?" Rob asked trying to understand. "W're they mean to ya?"

"No, they w're great." Alan replied. "I like 'em a lot. I miss 'em too."

"So, what hap'ened then?"

There was a solemn pause. Alan walked with his head down. "You." He answered sincerely without raising his head.

"Me?" Rob was shocked.

"I like you bett'r," Alan finally said.

"But you just met me. You don't even know me really."

"I know you well enough. Besides. You don't know me eith'r, but you missed me when I was gone, didn't ya?"

Rob couldn't argue with that. "Then come stay with me and Ma Ethel. She won't mind. You don't have to sleep outdoors."

"I 'on't know 'bout that," Alan said. "We'll see." Then he thought about the Marshalls and the promise he made to them. "Maybe one day you can meet 'em."

"Meet who?" Rob asked.

"Da folks I was stayin' with. They w're pretty sad when I left. I promised I'd come back to visit. Maybe you can go with me."

"Sure. I'd be glad ta."

#

Ethel had a long talk with Alan during dinner. He agreed to let her enroll him in school. He wouldn't commit to lodging with them just yet though. As crazy as he was about Rob, his trust issues wouldn't let him connect with Ethel.

Ethel didn't have any of the vital papers she needed to get him into school. Alan didn't share with her about the last school he attended when he was with the Marshalls. And he wasn't sure how old he really was. The school tested him to see where he stood academically. They three were all happy when he tested at the ninth-grade level. Now he could attend school with Rob.

When Ethel got him registered for school, somehow the word got out that he spent the summer living under a trestle. Neither of them could figure out how. They were careful not to mention that tidbit of information to anyone. Rob tried diligently to convince Alan to stay with them, but he couldn't just yet. Alan had left his home, wherever that was, to be near him. Rob felt responsible for him. Alan was content with just being near Rob for now. For some crazy reason, moving on wasn't on his agenda anymore.

3

PRETTIEST GIRL IN SCHOOL

§

Rob needed to tell Michelle something about Alan's condition. But he wasn't sure how. He shared that with Chasidy when she brought him lunch. "Any changes with Al?" Chasidy asked.

"Not yet. I don't know what to say to Mic."

Chasidy wanted to be there to help Mic the way that she has always been there for her. Neither Michelle nor AJ had seen Alan since they've been there. She needed to know something. "You want me to help?" she volunteered.

"If you can," Rob agreed.

"I can. We have to tell 'er somethan'. Knowan' a little bit of bad news is betta than not knowan' anythang at all. She needs to hear somethan about his condition. R'member when she and I w're missan'? Not knowan' was da worst part."

"Yeah. That's right," he agreed.

They settled Caitlin, Sam, and the babies in the private waiting area. Then proceeded on to visit with Mic and AJ. Chasidy stopped him. "Rob, I'll need to see 'im." That was the one thing Rob was trying to shield everyone from. He was a different Al. One, none of them were accustomed to.

He tried to prepare her. Suddenly, he remembered Al's and Ethel's warning. "Alright," he reached for her hand, "come with me."

She braced herself for the worst. She had to do this for her friend. Tears immediately formed in her eyes as she opened the curtains, but she held them back as she approached the bed. She hugged him for a long time and kissed him on the cheek. "If I had known you w're gonna do all this for a kiss, I would've defied Rob two years ago." Barlow chuckled at that. "Yor wife and son are going stir crazy. They're worried sick about you. They miss you. And they're scared b'cause they haven't seen you since y'all been h're." She touched his hand to hold it. "Now I'm gonna go tell them that yur doin betta. And you wanna see them too. Don't make me out to be a liar. Ok?" He squeezed her hand. She shrieked.

"What is it?" Rob asked.

"It felt like... She looked at Barlow smiling. "He squeezed my hand," she answered.

The thought of his family being worried about him hit a nerve. He squeezed her hand in reaction. He never wants to make them worry about anything. From the first time he saw Michelle, he thought of nothing but making her happy. He knew she would be his wife someday even as an adolescent. Childhood memories of Michelle danced around in his head. The day he declared her his wife before they had even met. And their journey along the bumpy road to get there.

§

They were headed out of Amory Benson High school on their way home one day. Al and Rob were just reaching the sidewalk when she came bursting through the doors, running out of the building to catch her ride. Alan watched her run to the car. "There she is Rob. Da prettiest girl in school. She's gon be my wife one day," he told him.

"You'll nev'r get her to turn you a look," Rob said. "She can have any boy in this school, why would she waste her time with a free roam'r like you?"

"She'll turn me a look," Alan said with confidence. "I'll accept yor apology on our weddin' day."

"Aren't you too young to be thinkin' bout marryin'?" Rob asked him.

"You sound like a' ol man," Alan replied. "I ain't thinkin' 'bout doin it t'morr'w. But some day." He smiled at the pleasing thought. Alan has always been very sure of what he wanted out of life. Family. At thirteen, he was now sure he wanted Michelle as part of his family.

§

Alan also smiled in his mind at the thought of his first love. His only love actually. From the moment he saw Mic, every other girl in the universe disappeared. They became soft blurs of pigmentations in the distance. In Chasidy's excitement over Alan's response, she encouraged him to do it again. She invited Rob over to the bed. Then she placed his hand in Rob's hand. "Al, if you can hear me, try to squeeze Rob's hand."

At first he was lost in the past with the memories of his first meeting of Michelle. He didn't honor Chasidy's request. But then his friend spoke to him, "Hey Buddy, if you can hear my voice, squeeze my hand." He remembered how Rob was always there for him when they were boys. How he never ceased to take care of him. No matter what. He squeezed his hand at his request as he continued his journey slowly back in time.

§

As they got closer to Rob's house, Alan said his goodbyes and turned towards the railroad trestle. "Why do you do this every day?" Rob asked him in frustration.

"Do what?" Al asked.

Rob looked at him with a convicting glare. "You know yur hungry. And you know Ma Ethel got dinn'r ready for us."

"For you," Al corrected. "She got dinn'r ready for you."

"And you too, Al. She makes sure she fixes enough for you too. When you don't come home with me to eat, she makes me come back out to get you. Doesn't she?" Well, I'm not comin' back out to get you ta'day. I got too much homework ta do." Rob scolded.

"You mean you'd let me starve?" Alan asked disappointedly.

"You'll let yorself starve. And you gon' starve t'night cause I'm – NOT – comin' - back - out - ta - get - you." Rob repeated once more very slowly.

"Some friend you are," Al replied, pretending to be upset. He knew Ma Ethel had cooked plenty. She always does. He just didn't feel right inviting himself to dinner. But Rob sounded like he meant what he said. And he is pretty hungry. "Well, maybe I will have dinn'r with you. Thanks for invitin' me ov'r," he said grinning coyly. "Why do you call 'er Ma Ethel?" He asked, changing the subject.

"Cause that's 'er name," Rob answered. "What else am I gonna call 'er?"

"I 'ont know. I thought kids just said mom or mama or somethin' like that," he said.

"Well," Rob started, "she's not my first mom."

"What's that mean?" Alan asked in confusion.

"My first mom died when I was real young. She and Ma Ethel w're best friends. Like us. She took me in and raised me for 'er own son." Rob explained.

"So yur an orphan? Like me," Alan said a little too excitedly for Rob.

"I ain't no orphan," Rob quickly corrected. "You don't have to be eith'r. Ma Ethel don't mind havin' two sons." Alan pondered that thought as they neared the house. "You need to come on and stay with us."

They entered the house through the kitchen door where Ethel was piddling around. She reached for Rob to extend him a hug. "Boys, yur in early. That's good! Alan, I'm glad I didn't have to send Robert back out for ya." She reached for a hug from him as well. He slowly obliged. Then she kissed him on the forehead. "I'm glad you came. Go get cleaned up and have a seat. Dinner's ready." Ethel said.

"Yes Mam. I wasn't going to at first. But he talked me inta comin' home with 'im." Al said.

"That's wonderful, Dear." she said. "I'm glad he did.

"Yeah, I told 'im I wasn't comin' back out to get 'im taday cause I had too much homework to do," Rob explained what Alan was really saying.

"What about you Alan. Do you have homework?" Ethel asked.

"Yes Mam," he answered politely.

"Well why don't you stay with Robert and you two can do yor homework t'gether?" Ethel was determined to win him over. Even though Alan was playing hardball.

"Maybe. I'll think about it," Alan said, thinking again about the conversation he and Rob just had. Ethel sat a big bowl of red beans and rice in front of him with a huge chunk of her sweet cornbread and some ice-cold tea. Alan was about to dive in but then he remembered, Ethel always says grace first. She smiled approvingly at him.

When they were nearly done with their dinner, Ethel told Rob about her visits today. He was a vital part of her neighborhood ministry to care for the elderly. But she made it clear to everyone that while school is in session, his schoolwork would come first. She enjoyed watching him be a child goofing off with Alan this past summer. But by doing so, the community has suffered the consequences for it. But they too were okay with Rob being a child for a change. However, there were things that needed to be done before the cold weather set in. Aside from helping with firewood, she didn't want him galivanting around in the cold. She stepped into the living room to grab her list. "These folks need yor help Robert," she said reaching him the list.

Rob's eyes lit up when he saw the list of work to be done. Ms Naples had a broken table that needed repairing. Old Man Collins needed his fence mended. And Mrs. Thomas wanted a screen door hung on the back porch. "Thanks Ma." Rob loved keeping his hands busy, building, and fixing things. But mostly building. And the extra pennies he earned sometimes were rewarding too. His list was a little bigger this time. Folks were becoming accustomed to his work.

"Don't thank me," she said. "Thank da good Lord and ya neighbors." She began clearing the table. "There's one more that's not on that list. He's comin' by in a few minutes to talk to ya in person. He wouldn't tell me what it was though."

"Who is it?" Rob asked.

"Sanderford," she said excitedly.

"Mr. Sanderford?" Rob repeated with the most surprised look on his face. "I wond'r what he wants."

Ethel heard his truck pull up into the yard. "Looks like we're about to find out. Come on inta da livin' room. We'll do dishes lat'r."

She greeted Mr. Sanderford and ushered him into the living room where Rob and Alan were waiting. They made their salutations, after which Mr. Sanderford got right to the point of his visit. "Son, I've been watchin' you doin little odd jobs all around town. People say nothin' but good things about yor work." Rob listened attentively. He felt something good was coming. "My granddaught'r is comin' ta stay with me in a month or so. I'd like to do somethin' special with 'er room. I'm gonna need a little bit of help with that. I was wonderin' if you might be interested in helpin' me?"

"Yes Sir, Mr. Sanderford!" Rob spoke almost before Sanderford could get the question out. But the responsibility he felt for Alan immediately surfaced.

"Young man I like yor enthusiasm. But you should nev'r agree to a job unless you feel good about da pay. You don't even know what I'm offerin'."

"I'm sure you'll be fair Mr. Sanderford," Rob answered. "B'sides I'd be good with any pay that would help Ma Ethel out." Sanderford liked that answer. Just then Rob noticed Alan was about to leave. "Where're you goin'?" Rob asked.

"Home," Alan answered, "ta get started on my homework."

"Mr. Sanderford," Rob said, "could you use one more person? I 'on't mind sharin' da pay."

"B'tween ya Mama and ya friend, that's not gonna leave much for you." Mr. Sanderford answered. The community watched him grow up in Ethel's care. He never really connected with any of the neighborhood children. That made everyone take notice of his instant connection to Alan. Especially when he all but stopped doing odd jobs and began hanging out with him.

"I understand that Sir," he told Sanderford.

Sanderford gave the boys a good looking over. He admired Ethel for taking in the boys and caring for them as her own. All they needed now was a little positive male influence. He didn't mind contributing that. "Well. As long as he's willing to work as hard as you do, yur both welcome. Here's what I'll do. I'll pay ya both $1.50 an hour. And each of you will give Ms Ethel yor .50 cents per hour for lettin' ya work for me. Does that sound fair?" he asked the boys. That was more money than Rob had made on any of his other jobs, and more than Alan had ever made.

"Yes Sir!" they both answered excitedly.

"Ms. Middleton?" he directed his attention to Ethel.

"Sounds fair enough to me," she answered. "Same rules apply though, aft'r schoolwork is done."

"I wouldn't have it any oth'r way," Sanderford agreed. "You know where I live, Rob. Come on ov'r when yor schoolwork is done. We'll get started right away."

"Yes Sir," they answered again excitedly.

Alan couldn't believe Rob had included him in this deal. He has never had a friend before. Especially not one who felt like a brother.

Later on, Rob noticed Alan doing more thinking than homework. "You must be spendin' da night t'night?" he asked Al.

"Huh," Alan answered.

"What w're you thinkin' about? You w're a million miles away," Rob said.

"How come you did that?" he asked his friend.

"Did what?"

"How come you got me work with you?"

Rob looked confused. "What? You don't wanna work?"

"I didn't say that." Alan defended.

"Whatta you sayin' then?" Rob asked.

"I'm just wonderin' why you thought about me like that. That's all. You could've made all that money for you and ya mama." Alan replied.

"You ain't got nothin'. You can use some money too." Rob said.

"Just don't be thinkin' I'm some ol' beggar or somethin'." Alan told him.

"Quit being stupid, Al." Rob said. "I know yur tough enough. Nobody's givin' you nothin'. We both being paid." But somehow Rob knew what Alan was really trying to say. He knew he appreciated him thinking of him and giving him a chance to work and make his own money. He knew that he was really trying to say thanks. "Yur welcome," he said lastly.

They quickly finished their homework and Rob convinced Alan they should do their small projects first. The faster they were done, the sooner they could get started on the big job with Mr. Sanderford. Ethel was happy Alan was working with Rob. It was a good opportunity to encourage him to stay with them. She put a bug in Alan's ear before he left. "You know, yur gonna be plenty tired when yur done with all this work Rob's got you caught up in. You'll be needin' a nice soft bed ta rest up in. That offer I made b'fore still stands. I have an extra room or an extra bed ta put in Rob's room. Yor choice." Alan didn't respond. He just smiled a semi-smile at Ethel as he and Rob left.

He asked Rob once they were outside, "How come yor Ma Ethel's so nice to me?"

"Cause she's a nice person," Rob answered. "How come yur so suspicious of everybody?"

"Cause I'm a suspicious person," Alan answered.

"You don't have to be suspicious of Ma," Rob said. "She likes you."

"She does?" Alan asked with a slightly raised voice.

"Yeah. Didn't she give you a sweet kiss on da forehead?" Alan smiled. "That's why she keeps askin' you to stay with us." Rob explained. "I wished you'd stay too and get out from und'r that trussell."

"I'll thank about it," Alan said.

"You always say that." Rob said. "Stop thinkin' so much. Just do it."

\#

Alan watched Rob work like a pro as he repaired the old table leg. Like he'd been doing this all his life. "How'd you learn how to do all this stuff?"

"I 'on't know. It's just in my head," Rob answered. "Like yor fishin' pole.

"You think you could teach me?"

"Sure. You taught me, didn't ya? It'll be easy. You already have it in yor head too." He started at that very moment explaining everything he was doing to the table leg preparing it to be put back onto the table. When he was done, it had to be left over night to dry. "We'll come back t'morrow ta put it back on da table." Alan hadn't mentioned anything about moving in with him and Ethel all day. On the way home, Rob brought it up. "So, what's yor answ'r?"

"To what?" Alan pretended he didn't know what Rob was talking about.

Rob wished his friend wouldn't make it so hard for people to care for him. "Ma really cares about you Al. You need to stop makin' 'er work so hard to show it."

As sincere as Rob sounded, Al still had a difficult time accepting that. "I 'on't know Rob," he said. "I 'on't know Ma Ethel."

"How come you trust me so much?" Rob asked him. "From da first time we met even."

"I 'on't know. It's just in my head. Like... I'm supposed to." Alan answered. "How come you took ta me so?"

Rob was taken aback by that question. Throwing it back at him like that, he understood. He had taken to him also. From day one. He thought he'd use the same phycology on him. "Then trust me when I tell you Ma Ethel really wants you to come live with us. Listen, yur nev'r gonna have a chance with that pretty girl as long as yur livin' und'r a railroad trussell." That got Alan to thinking. "And I really want ya ta move in with us too. I don't like you sleepin' outdoors like an animal. Yur my best friend. You don't have to do that."

That made Alan think even more. He knew Rob was his best friend, but it wasn't until that moment that he knew Rob felt exactly the same about him. "Well, if yur sure Ma Ethel don't mi ...."

"Great!" Rob said before Al could even finish his sentence. "Let's go tell 'er right now!"

Ethel was ecstatic. "That's wonderful!" she exclaimed. "Now I can take care-a you proper, Alan. You boys run on. Go get Alan's stuff and come right on back home."

"Home," Alan said. "I can call it that?"

"Call it that?" Rob asked. "If that's what Ma Ethel said, that's what Ma Ethel meant."

"That's what I said, Sweetheart," Ethel confirmed, "b'cause that's what it is."

#

By the time Alan and Rob finished their small projects and were ready to start working with Mr. Sanderford, Alan was already comfortable with his living arrangements with Rob and Ma Ethel. He had chosen to share Rob's room with him instead of having one to himself. Sometimes they spent half the night talking until one or both of them fell asleep.

Sanderford had listened to talk of Rob all over town about his work and how much care he took in it. Being retired from the carpentry trade himself, he was very impressed with what he heard, and saw. He wanted to use this opportunity to help Rob perfect his craftmanship. He was looking forward to the boys working with him. Rob's craftmanship, however, at the young age of fourteen, was mind boggling. "Son, have you been here b'fore in anoth'r lifetime?" he asked Rob.

"I 'on't know Sir. I 'on't think so," Rob answered, not realizing it was meant more for a compliment than a question. Working up close and personal with Alan, he noticed some pretty impressive abilities in him also.

They finished the project two weeks before his granddaughter was scheduled to arrive. Sanderford was so impressed with the boys, he kept finding things around the house for them to do to keep a little change in their pockets. "A man should always have his own money," he told them. He coached them on other things as well that a father would usually coach his son on. Ethel was a great mom, but Mr. Sanderford filled a gap few women are able to fill. They had great respect for him because of that.

But work and substitute fatherhood was halted after his granddaughter arrived. She was living with her grandmother, her dad's mother, when she became ill. Both of her parents were already deceased. She didn't want to leave her grandmother. She wanted to stay and take care of her. But all involved agreed it was too much for a fourteen-year-old child. Her grandmother was placed in an elderly care facility, and she was shipped off to live with her grandpa.

The halt in work worked out fine for Alan and Rob. They had worked diligently and earned enough money to buy new outfits for the Fall Harvest Festival Dance. Alan would finally get a chance to meet the prettiest girl in school, Michelle Peterson. He had his work cut out for him. Many of the popular football players had already been competing for her attention. He never really saw her hanging out with any of them at school though.

Ethel could see that they were both nervous as they readied themselves for the event. "Who's da lucky girl, or girls?" she asked.

Alan tried to hide it from her. "There ain't no girls Mam." he said.

"Boy, you'd have come out bett'r tellin' me you w're headed to da moon," Ethel said smiling. "All these jitters b'tween da two of ya have girls scribbled all ov'r 'em."

Rob wasn't a snitch, but he was all tickled inside about Al liking Michelle. He was bursting to tell it. "Al has a crush on da prettiest girl in da school. He's hopin' she's gon be there t'night."

"Rob!" Alan objected.

Ethel giggled. She perfectly understood the effects of first crush jitters, she wanted to send him away with all the confidence he could carry in that unpretentious little mind of his. She went into her bedroom and came back with a handheld mirror. "Smile," she said. He gave her a half-hearted one. She tickled his tummy. He burst into laughter. When she held the mirror to his face, she asked, "What girl in 'er right mind can ignore this smile on a face with those eyes?" she asked. "If she does, she's not da girl for you. Go, have fun!"

#

That was easier said than done. The walk there was more comfortable than the dance itself. He knew some of the kids knew he used to stay under the trestle. He felt like everyone there knew by now. He had to get passed that before he could even think about enjoying himself or asking Michelle to dance with him. Rob spent most of the evening encouraging him. But his nerves were hiding from him like he used to hide from the grownups at Chiricahua.

Her hair was in a ponytail. The same as any other day. He imagined what she looked like with it down touching her pretty face. Then he imagined getting close enough to her to let it down himself. That thought brought a smile to his face. He wondered if that smile looked the same as the one in Ma Ethel's mirror.

Rob on the other hand was having a ball. He just danced. And any girl on the floor that wanted to dance with him, did so. Alan finally got the nerve to follow his friend's lead. It wasn't long before he too was surrounded by pretty dancers. He was actually enjoying himself, but not as much as he could have if his nerves would cooperate with him.

The dance would be over at ten o'clock. Ten o'clock was fifteen minutes away and he still hadn't danced with Michelle. The only girl in the room he really wanted to dance with. *'It's now or never'*, he thought. He walked slowly over to where she was standing with some other popular girls. She noticed him walking in their direction. She watched him the whole time, thinking how cute he looked all dressed up. "Hi," he said nervously. "Would you... mind... dancin'... with me?"

Before Michelle could answer, one of the other girls spoke to him, "Hey, aren't you that homeless boy that live und'r da railroad track?"

"Yeah, da trussell rat?" another one added.

"What?" Alan asked embarrassed, as he looked at the girls. Then he looked back at Michelle. She didn't say anything. She waited to hear his answer. He didn't answer. Instead, he turned to walk away, thinking, maybe Rob was right, maybe he didn't have a chance with her after all. But then he thought about what Ethel said. If she can ignore my smile, she's not da girl for me. Deep in his heart, he felt she was. But he just had to find out for sure. He envisioned the smile from Ethel's mirror and plastered it on to his face. Then turned back around and asked her, "Have you ev'r danced with a trussell rat b'fore?"

"No. And I'm not about to start now," Michelle said. The other girls thought that was funny. Alan once again started slowly walking away as the girls laughed at him. Then he heard Michelle speak again. "But I will dance with you, Amber Eyes." The girls stopped laughing immediately. They looked at Michelle like she was committing a major high school crime. But Michelle didn't care. She thought Alan had the handsomest eyes she had ever seen. She wanted to be friends with the boy they belonged to.

They made their real introductions to each other, then laughed, and talked for the rest of the evening. She didn't seem the least bit bothered by him being the boy who lived under the trussell. So, he wasn't bothered either. He spent the last fifteen minutes of the Fall Harvest Festival Dance dancing with the prettiest girl in school.

4

TRESTLE RAT

§

Rob looked at Chasidy smiling, "Go get da nurse." Alan was still holding his hand with a very firm grip when the team came in.

"He squeezed your hand, your wife said?"

"Yes. Her's first and then mine," Barlow explained.

"Step back please. Let us get to 'im." One of the nurses said.

"I can't. He won't let go of my hand," Barlow told them. "Hey Buddy, these people need to take a look at you. They need me to move outta da way. You need to let go of my hand for me to do that. Okay. I won't go anywhere. I promise."

He knew he wouldn't. Rob had stood by him all of their days. Especially when the kids at school were a little less than friendly to him. At that comforting thought, he released his friend's hand and went back to that melancholy time in his childhood. The staff watched as Alan loosened his grip.

§

Once the wind took hold of Alan's interest in Michelle carrying it through the halls of the school, some of the students (namely the popular varsity players who thought she was better suited for one of them) vowed to make him rethink his interests. One in particular, Junior Green, whose given name is Dunbar after his dad, made it his personal quest to make Al's life at school the worst life possible. He liked Michelle too and he thought Michelle shared his sentiment until Alan came along. Alan wasn't one to back down from a challenge even if that challenge was in the form of a fight. Somehow the words 'trussell rat' always led to a fight. Rob wasn't about to let Alan face a challenge or a fight alone.

Practically on a daily basis Junior would tease Alan about spending the summer under the trestle and purposely on purpose calling him 'trussell rat' whenever he saw him and Michelle together. Most times Alan tried to ignore him and his bullying friends who were with him. But Junior didn't make it very easy for him. What Junior didn't know was that the more he teased and taunted Alan; the more cool points he lost with Michelle.

It was starting to bother Alan. And what bothered Alan, bother Rob. One afternoon after their homework was done, Rob and Alan decided to go fishing to take their minds off of the torment Alan had to deal with at school. When they got there, it did anything but that. Because what they saw made them even angrier. It was bad enough that Junior Green and his gang were constantly in his face at school. But now they were in his pond too. Butt naked it appeared because they saw clothes scattered all over the ground. Junior saw them walking up to the pond with their fishing poles. "Hey guys, look who's comin'. I bet they fish h're all da time. Let's pee in da water to make their fish taste bett'r." They all laughed while giving a sigh of relief like they had just urinated in the water.

"Dumb Bar, that makes about as much sense as you idiots swimming butt naked in the middle of Fall." Rob said.

"Yeah. And leaving yor clothes fair game for anybody walking by," Alan added. He began picking their clothes up off the ground. Rob realized what he was doing and helped him.

"Hey! Those are our clothes!" One of the guys yelled. "Putt 'em back!"

"Get out and make us," Alan said. "You may think you run da school, but yur on our home field now." He spoke a language they could understand. Alan had a point. They were protected in school. So, they didn't get out of the water. They just yelled obscenities at them. And told them what they would do to them if they didn't put their clothes back. Alan and Rob took their clothes but then wondered what to do with them on their way back to the house.

As they walked, Rob remembered they had to pass Connie Calloway's house. Better known as Connie the Carnivore because like Junior, she loved eating her fellow classmates alive. They made certain no one was watching and neatly spread the clothes across the fence.

It was still daylight out and they couldn't get out of the water for fear of someone seeing them naked. They had to wait until dark. The air was starting to turn cool. And so did their bodies. When they finally got out of the pond near frozen to icicles, they ran in the direction Alan and Rob went to look for their clothes. They found them on the Carnivore's fence. It was by a sheer stroke of luck that the Carnivore was out with her parents and just arriving home as the naked boys were trying to retrieve their clothes from her fence. They couldn't explain what they were doing there. They wouldn't dare admit that the Rat had outwitted them.

Every other week it seemed Alan and Rob were getting expelled from school. Even though Junior and the others were the instigators. One would have thought that they might have learned their lesson from the pond incident. They did. They never step foot back on their turf again. But they knew they had dominant reign at school with the principal in their corner. And Junior had sworn an oath to make Alan's life completely miserable. He intended to hold to that oath.

Ethel had little success convincing the school of the unfairness that portrayed to her boys. Principal Jenson backed his varsity team one hundred percent. It was clear that Alan and Rob were on their own when it came to school faculty. So, they handled matters the only way they knew how, standing their ground.

Michelle, Alan, and Rob were having lunch together in the cafeteria this particular day when Alan had decided he had had just about enough of

Junior. He didn't know what Junior had up his sleeves when he saw him coming, but Alan had vowed to himself that whatever Junior started, he was going to finish it today once and for all. Sure enough, Junior started in on Alan with his teasing and name calling. "Hey trussell rat. I thought you might be missin' yor family, so I brought you a visitor. He wants to have lunch with ya." He held a brown bag over Alan's tray and dumped a dead rat on top of Alan's food. Michelle started screaming along with some of the other girls and moving away from the table. Junior and his friends started laughing hysterically at Alan.

Alan stayed remarkably calm looking at the rat on his plate. When he stood up, Rob stood up with him. "You look hungry, Junior," he said to the boy who was nearly twice his size. "I'm gonna share my food with you taday."

Junior stopped laughing. "And just how do you plan to do that, RAT?" Rob stood between Alan and the boys who were with Junior to make certain it would be a fair fight. "Just whatta you think yur doin? You don't really think I need help beatin' da crap outta this rat, do ya?"

Rob never let Alan fight Junior before because of their size difference. But he knew today, this was Alan's fight. He had to be the one to put an end to Junior's foolery. He also knew that Alan had come to the end of his rope with Junior which made him well capable of doing it. "Al's tough enough," Rob said to him.

While Junior was talking to Rob, Alan picked up his tray and slammed it into Junior's face. It knocked him to the floor. When he fell to the floor, he picked up the rat and shoved it into his mouth. "Since you like rats so much," Alan said, "have one for lunch." Alan was sitting with his entire body on Junior, shoving the rat into his mouth until he started gagging. Then he started hitting him in the face. "Yur gonna leave me alone, Dumb Bar! Yur gonna stop teasin' me and yur gonna stop callin' me a trussell rat or I'm gonna make you eat da rest of his family's rat meat too!"

By the time Principal Jenson had gotten there, it was Alan who had beaten the crap out of Junior who still had the rat sticking out of his mouth. Amazingly enough, his friends didn't even try to go through Rob to help him. Principal Jenson, in his own version of fairness, once again only suspended Alan and Rob.

#

When the boys told Ethel about it, she became furious, but she didn't know what she could do about it. It seemed that school was dead set against her boys who really weren't bad boys at all. She spoke to Mr. Sanderford about it and hoped he had some helpful suggestions. He asked her to send the boys over. He wanted to hear from them what was going on in their own words.

Alan was reluctant to talk at first. And Rob didn't want to be a tattle-tell. "I can't help if I don't know what's going on." Sanderford told them.

The boys sat quietly on the sofa across from Mr. Sanderford's chair. Alan looked at Rob as if asking for advice. "Go ahead Al. Tell 'im," Rob said.

"They think it's funny bein' homeless," Alan started after a slight pause.

"He ain't homeless no more," Rob added.

"They call me a trussell rat." Alan told him humbly.

"Al ain't no rat either," Rob told him angrily.

"They're always pickin' fights with me, tellin' me to go back where I come from. I 'on't both'r them," Alan continued. "When they push me, I push 'em back. I ain't no chicken, just like I ain't no rat."

"I'm not gonna let Al take a beatin from em," Rob added. "Al can whoop da lot of 'em in a fair fight. But they don't fight fair."

"I see," Sanderford said. "You boys plan to fight all yor life every time somebody says somethin' you don't like?" he asked them.

"No," Alan said. "We 'on't wanna fight."

Rob helped him out, "Whatta we supposed to do? Take a beatin'? I'm supposed to let Al take a beatin'?"

"Fightin' isn't da answer to anythin'. You boys are smart'r than that. With da stuff that comes outta yor heads, da two of you outta be able to come up with a bett'r way to handle this."

The boys were disappointed. They were thinking Sanderford had turned on them too. "Al handled it well enough today," Rob said. "I on't think Junior or anybody else is gonna both'r him anymore."

"Why is that?" Mr. Sanderford asked.

"Junior put a dead rat in my food," Alan told him. "I wasn't even through eatin'."

"Where'd da rat come from?" Sanderford asked.

"Junior brought it to school with 'im," Rob answered. "But Al fixed 'im up right."

"What'd you do, Al?"

"I fed it to 'im. Shoved it right down his throat." Sanderford chuckled before he realized it. But quickly collected himself, not wanting to condone those kinds of actions. "Then Principal Jenson suspended us. Rob didn't even touch anybody." Alan said.

Mr. Sanderford wasn't ignorant to what goes on in school. He remembers bullying all too well from his school days. And this has gone way too far and gotten too far out of hand. "I'll tell you what, you boys promise me you'll try yor best to ignore these bozos from now on and I'll back you up against da school when push comes to shove, and you have no oth'r choice but to defend yorself. Okay?"

Al and Rob looked at each other with hope. That's really what they were doing anyway. "Okay, Mr. Sanderford," both boys said.

In the meantime, he decided to have a talk with Principal Jenson when he went to enroll Becky in school. That was supposed to be next week, but if Jenson hadn't suspended the boy who started this mess, he was determined Alan and Rob weren't spending a single day at home either.

Just then Sanderford's granddaughter entered the room. Both boys noticed her right away. "Boys, I'd like ya ta meet my granddaught'r Becky. Becky these are da boys I told you about who helped me with yor room. Rob and Al."

Rob's eyes were instantly glued to her, but it was Alan who spoke first. "Hello."

She returned the greeting, "Hi. You guys did a wonderful job. Thank you. I love my room." Focusing her attention on Rob, she then asked, "Don't you have any manners? Aren't you gonna speak?" She didn't talk like them. Like Southerners. Her voice was soft and sweet. Her mannerism was poised and graceful, like a southern bell. But not.

Coming out of his daze, he spoke softly, "Hello."

Then she immediately turned to Mr. Sanderford, "Grandpa, I'm ready when you are," she said referring to their outing in the park they had planned earlier in the week.

"Becky will be starting school next week. Make sure she feels welcome." Sanderford told them. Then he said to Becky, "There's been a change in plans, Sweetheart. We've gotta make a run to da school." Then he called Ethel to let her know he was coming to pick her up.

#

Sanderford was one of the big names in the community. He was a huge supporter of the athletic department in the school. His daughter attended Amory Benson and he was happy his granddaughter would be attending also. But Sanderford was a firm believer that all children should be treated equally. He was determined to even the playing field for Al and Rob whom he had deemed his boys. He had hoped they could find a suitable fix for Alan's dilemma. That was easier said than done.

The principal had heard in the wind that his granddaughter was coming to live with him. He was thrilled to see them both entering his office. "Mr. Sanderford, so good to see ya. Are you bringing us a new student?" the principle asked him smiling down at Becky.

"If you'll have 'er," Sanderford answered. Then he said, "Let's talk a minute b'fore you meet 'er."

They entered the office after which the principal closed the door behind them. Sanderford got right to the point. "Mr. Jenson I'm concerned about a couple of boys who got suspended for fightin' taday."

Mr. Jenson immediately cut him off. "A couple of troublemakers those two are. What's yor concern? Have they done somethin'?" he asked.

"No. I just don't like..."

Mr. Jenson cut him off again, "If yur worried about them botherin' yor granddaughter, I can assure you she'll be perfectly safe." The principal promised.

"Actually, I was more concerned...." The principal cut Sanderford off for a third time. Sanderford just sat back at this point and listened to the principle bad mouthing his boys.

"Now don't you be concerned about a thing. Those two are gonna fight themselves right outta school. I'm not gonna put up with their disruption in school for much long'r. Ms. Middleton had the gall to insinuate that the school was being unfair to them. I'll tell you what she needs to do, she needs to find a positive male role model ta teach those two how to act in society. She says the guys on the football team are the ones really causing the trouble. I'll put that little trussell rat and his friend outta school for good before I suspend anyone on my team." The Principle declared.

Sanderford was finally able to get a full sentence out, which came in the form of a question. "What exactly did da boys do taday?" Mr. Jenson twisted the entire story and blamed everything on Alan and Rob. Even the part about bringing a rat to school. He never once mentioned that the other boys started this whole thing by picking on Alan and had been since Alan started school. "Jenson, yur eith'r as dumb as a box of rocks or yur showing a whole lotta favoritism. Somethin' that's got no place in school. Cause that's not da story I heard. In fact, you've been twisting stories ever since Alan started school. The kids have been bullyin' him all year and you haven't done a thing about it. Not only that, but nobody ev'r got sent home except da two of 'em. Why exactly is that?"

"You sound like Ms. Middleton, Mr. Sanderford. What's yor interest in this anyway?" Mr. Jenson asked, purposely neglecting to answer his question.

Sanderford chuckled a little. "Well, you see, I kinda like ta think of myself as that positive male influence you spoke of earlier." Mr. Jenson suddenly ran out of words. "I haven't liked what I've heard h're taday so far. Yur da principal. Yur supposed to treat every child in this school equally. Clearly you haven't done that with Alan and Robert." Sanderford wanted Mr. Jenson to know that he was well aware of what happened in the cafeteria today. "Here's da real story, Jenson. Alan was minding his own business having his lunch when Junior Green walked up and put a dead rat on his tray. That's what started da fight. If anybody should've been suspended, it should've been Junior. He doesn't deserve to walk away from this unpunished."

"If I suspend Junior, you'll have a fight on yor hands with his father for sure," Jenson argued.

Sanderford chuckled softly. "The funny thing about that is, he'll have that same fight with me," Sanderford replied. "You might even look into da rest of da team's b'havior. They need to know this type-a b'havior won't be tolerated h're."

"Well just what would you have me do, Mr. Sanderford, suspend my whole football team?"

"If yor whole football team is causin' da trouble," Sanderford said. "But what you certainly don't do is help them demeanor another child. Alan doesn't pick fights. I know that ta be a fact. You owe those boys and Ms. Middleton an apology. Her boys deserves to be safe h're at school just like everyone else. Now whatta you gonna do to make that hap'en?"

"Yur askin' me to choose b'tween my star football player and two..."

"Choose yor next words carefully," Sanderford warned, interrupting him this time. "I'm not askin' you anythin'. I'm tellin' you yur gonna make this right for my boys. Yur gonna put yor team in check. They're gonna stop callin' Alan a trussell rat. And they're gonna leave my boys alone. Or yor team will be spendin' more time holdin' fundraisers than playin' football cause da school will nev'r get anoth'r red cent of my money for its athletic department. In da meantime, Alan and Rob are in da hallway waitin' ta return to class aft'r yor sincere apology. And I expect every suspension you've given them to be erased off their record effective taday," Mr. Sanderford spoke calmly but firmly.

"Now, Mr. Sanderford, don't be hasty. We rely heavily on da community's support ...."

Mr. Sanderford interrupted him again, "Then I suggest you get to work correctin' this matt'r."

With much reluctance, Mr. Jenson instructed the secretary to bring Ms. Middleton and the boys into his office. Sanderford sat quietly from that point on to see how the conversation would go. He knew Mr. Jenson didn't feel any remorse for the way he treated Alan and Rob. He just didn't want to lose critical financial support. However, he did apologize to the three of them for neglecting to run his school in an unbiased manner. Ethel accepted his apology but was more concerned about retaliation from the other boys. "How can I be certain they won't do somethin' ta hurt 'em?" she asked.

Principal Jenson instructed his secretary once more. This time to call Junior and the other two boys to his office. When they entered, their eyes met with Mr. Sanderford's. They knew him well and were well aware of his contributions to the school's athletic department. They've thanked him many times for that. They wondered what his association with Alan and Rob was.

The principal informed Junior that he'll be put on suspension for the next three days and ordered the boys to apologize to Alan and Rob. He also made it clear to them that their behavior towards them had to stop. He assured them that they would face more consequences if it continued.

"My dad's not gonna like this!" Junior blurted out.

"Then he can come see me," Principal Jenson said. Then he sent all of the boys back to their classes. But not before the boys also apologized to Alan and Rob.

While he was there, Sanderford registered Becky for school and he and Ethel returned home. Ethel was grateful. All she wanted was for her boys to be safe and treated fairly. "I am forev'r in yor debt," she told Sanderford. "My boys are good boys."

"Yes they are. And blessed to have you in their lives," he agreed. "There's no debt h're though. It's all small grains of sand b'tween family," Sanderford said to her.

"Family?" she asked in shock.

"Yep, when yor Rob looked at my Becky taday, I could've sworn I heard weddin' bells in da distance." They both laughed.

"Well, he's got good taste. She certainly is a lovely girl," Ethel said. "But not until his schooling's done," she said still laughing.

"I wouldn't have it any oth'r way, Ms. Middleton," Sanderford agreed.

#

On the boy's walk home from school, Rob hardly said a word to Alan. Alan knew why. Their relationship had already progressed to a point where they could usually tell when the other had something on his mind. Sometimes, even what the other was thinking. He began to teased him about it. "You like 'er, don't ya?"

"Like who?" Rob asked.

"Quit playin' dumb," Alan said.

Rob looked at Alan smiling, "Michelle may be da prettiest girl in school," he said, "but Becky is da prettiest girl in da whole world."

"You ain't seen all da girls in da world," Alan told him.

"It don't matt'r. Wherev'r I go, I won't ev'r see nobody prettier than she is."

#

Ethel had invited Sanderford and Becky over for dinner to thank him for his help today. They were all just about done eating when they heard a couple of vehicles pull up in the yard. "Sanderford! Get out h're! We wanna talk to you." Dunbar Sr. yelled for him. All three fathers came to give Sanderford a good talking to.

"You boys stay h're with ya Ma and Becky," he told Alan and Rob.

"No way Mr. Sanderford, I can't do that," Rob told him. "They can't come h're and be disr'spectful at Ma Ethel's house. Not ta her, Al, or you."

"Yeah," Alan added. "All this started with me. It's gonna end with me. I'm done bein' picked on."

Sanderford admired the boys even more for being willing to stand their ground with grown men. "Let's go see what they're sayin'," he told them. He walked out on the porch. Everybody followed him. Ethel wasn't leaving her boys to face the wolves alone. "What's da problem Dunbar?" Sanderford asked.

"Da problem is my boy's gotta miss three days outta school b'cause of you! He says you got 'im suspended!" An angry Dunbar Green spoke.

"And how exactly did he say I did that?" Sanderford asked him. "It's my understandin' that a child can't get suspended unless he did somethin' ta get suspended for."

"He said these two lied on 'im and you helped 'em and that's why he got suspended!" Mr. Green lashed at him.

"Green, I can see from what yur tellin' me, you don't have a clue about what's goin' on here. Maybe you should sit down with yor boy and ask 'im for da truth. Maybe all of ya should do that." Sanderford told him and the other dads who were with him.

"Are you callin' my boy a liar?" Mr. Green asked him.

Sanderford chuckled. "You mean like what you just did ta my boys and me?" Sanderford spoke calmly but definitely. "Alan, why don't you tell Mr. Green da truth about his son."

"I don't need to hear nothin' from..." Mr. Green started to speak, but Rob interrupted him.

"You'll lis'en or you'll leave! Those da only two choices you have. I won't have you bein' disr'spectful in front of my mama. Especially at 'er own house. Or talkin' ta Mr. Sanderford that way! You can leave right now if you 'on't wanna hear what Alan's gotta say!" Rob spoke boldly like a grown-up man. Mr.

Green and the others stood there wondering what to make of the fourteen-year-old who dared to stand up to them. Then he told Alan, "They're still standin' h're, Al. Go ahead."

Alan didn't waste any time speaking up for himself. "Yor boy been pickin' at me since I started school cause I stayed und'r da railroad trussell 'til Ma Ethel and Rob let me stay with 'em. He and his friends thinks it's funny not havin' no home to stay in. Every day they call me a trussell rat and try to pick a fight. When we do fight, don't nobody get sent home but me and Rob. Taday at lunch, he brought a dead rat ta school. Said he was my family and put 'im on my lunch tray. I didn't even get to finish my lunch. I 'on't like wastin' food bein' homeless and all. So, I fed it to 'im. Jenson suspended us again. Rob didn't even fight this time. He didn't do nothin' ta yor boy and his friends. Til Mr. Sanderford brought us back to school. He don't nev'r do nothin' ta 'em. He should've been suspended a long time ago," Alan told him. "I ain't nev'r done nothin' ta him."

Mr. Green and the others weren't naive. They knew their boys had likely done something. They figured it was just boyish horseplay. But they were raised in church, encouraged to love, respect, and help others. It never entered their minds that they would do something like this. Mr. Green was furious at what he had just heard. "Is this true, Junior?" he asked his son. Junior upheld his original story. Then Mr. Green looked at the other boys. "Jason, Cody," he said. "Have y'all been tormentin' this boy all year?" The boys dropped their heads, and their fathers knew Alan had told them the truth. Turning back to Junior, Mr. Green was even angrier, "You straight faced lied to me, in front-a all these people!"

One of the other dads stepped up to the porch where Alan and Rob were standing. He reached his hand to Rob for a handshake. "Son, I admire you for standin' up for yor mama and yor friend like that. You keep that up." Then he looked past Alan and said to Sanderford, "I'm glad they had you to help 'em out. Ain't no tellin' how long this would've gone on oth'rwise." When he turned back to Alan, he just stood for a few seconds and stared at him. When he finally spoke, what he said shocked everybody. "Young man, can I give you a hug?" Alan stared back at him. "I have no idea what it's like to live und'r a railroad trussell. I couldn't pull that off even as a man. Yur one tough fella," he told Alan.

Alan replied, "I'm tough enough," before giving him the hug he asked for. Mr. Green and the other dad apologized as well and made their boys apologize too. For a second time.

"Mr. Sanderford, thank ya for bringin' this out in da light," Mr. Green said much calmer than when he arrived. "Ms. Middleton, I'm sorry for my boy's actions. I think I'll pull Junior off da team until he shows me he's learned somethin' from all-a this. I had no idea. I nev'r would've allowed this ta go on. I didn't raise 'im like that."

"Glad to hear it Mr. Green," Sanderford replied on Ethel's behalf.

Ethel was proud of the way her boys handled themselves. She realized that very day that they would grow up to conquer and not be conquered. The boys had proven what she and Sanderford both already knew; that they weren't hot-headed little boys who couldn't control their tempers. But that they respected others and expected the same respect from them.

\#

Before going to sleep Alan was deep in thought about what Mr. Sanderford had done for him today. And how the other parents came around to him. This place just keeps getting better and better to him. He has a home and a family who feels real to him. And now the town's people were accepting him too. The more he thought about it, the more he wanted to stay.

The room was dark, Alan was quiet. But Rob had a sense Al was meditating on something. "You woke?" he asked.

"Yeah," Alan replied.

"What are you thinkin' on?"

"How nice Mr. Sanderford is. How he helped me taday."

"Yeah, that was pretty nice of 'im," Rob agreed. "Did you see Junior's face when his dad said he was takin 'im off da team?"

"Yeah," they both laughed. "At first, I was tryin' to think of a way to get back at 'em somehow." Alan said. "Now I don't have to."

"You already got back at 'im anyway," Rob said.

"Whatta you mean?" he asked. "How?"

Rob began laying it out for him. "When you put that rat in his mouth, everybody in da cafeteria saw it. Then you gave 'im a proper beatdown. He had to be embarrassed by that." Rob told him. Then continued. "But I think more than that even, you stole his girl. That's what got 'im angry at you in da first place." Alan liked that answer better actually. He fell asleep with the biggest grin plastered on his face.

5

WHERE THE HEART IS

§

By now, Alan is lost deep in thought of his childhood. So much so, that when the hospital staff tried to get him to respond to them, he was too far away to oblige. They had come to a medical conclusion and explained to Barlow that Alan may be entering into a vegetative state that could last for weeks, months even. Alan wasn't even close to being a vegetable. He was very active in his reminiscing as his mind returned to pleasant thoughts of his wife in their younger days.

§

Michelle was glad to see Alan and Rob back at school yesterday. But mostly Alan. She wondered what happened that they were able to come back so soon. She didn't get the chance to talk to him because of their afternoon class schedule. She could hardly wait to see him today.

Alan was feeling anxious too for a different reason. Michelle had never seen him that angry before. He wasn't sure how she would receive him today. But he was about to find out. She was waiting outside the school for him to arrive. His anxiety left him when he saw her smiling and waving at him. She walked quickly to meet him. "Good morning Robert," she said.

"Good morning Michelle, Rob replied.

She grabbed Al's hand and started towards the school. "What? I don't get a good morning?" he asked.

"Good morning Al!"

"Good morning Mic," he said.

She walked back to the school with him and Rob full of inquisitiveness. "I'm glad yur back. Mr. Jenson can be so unfair ta you two. I hate it when he does that," she rambled on. "How'd y'all get ta come back yest'rday anyway?" she asked him.

Rob saw Mr. Sanderford's truck pullup, so he went to meet Becky. "I'll catch up with you lat'r, Al. Becky's h're," he said.

"Who's Becky?" Michelle asked.

"Mr. Sanderford's granddaught'r. Rob likes 'er," he said smiling. Then he said, "You sure have a lotta questions this mornin'."

"Yeah," she said, "and you've only answered one of 'em so far."

"Well," Alan started, "it's b'cause of that man right there."

"Mr. Sanderford? What'd he do?" Michelle asked him.

"I 'on't know exactly. I just know he brought us back to school yest'rday with Ma Ethel. He went in and had a talk with Mr. Jenson. Next thing I know, Mr. Jenson's apologizin' ta all of us. Then he made Junior 'em apologize too."

By now, they had made it to Michelle's classroom. "Well, I'm glad it all worked out. I'll see ya at lunch," she said entering her classroom.

Rob walked Becky to her classroom also. Once all the commotion was over with, on yesterday, he and Becky had a few minutes to talk and get to know one another. She had been impressed at how he dealt with the grownups. But she was even more impressed with how her grandfather was taken with him. He talked about him all evening right up until bedtime. "Rob Barlow!" she said.

"Good mornin' Becky, Mr. Sanderford," he spoke.

"Morning Son."

"Bye Grandpa!" Becky said waving good-bye. She and Rob started inside. She looked to both sides of his head. "I thought yor ears would be burned completely off," she said.

He was all too familiar with the old superstition of burning ears when someone is heavily talking about you. Ethel uses it all the time. "Why is that? You been talkin' 'bout me?" he asked her.

"Not me," she said. "Not that I didn't want to," hinting that she liked him. "I just couldn't get a word in edgewise for Grandpa rambling on about you. He sure is some kind of proud of you. He thinks the world of you and Alan. But mostly you."

That made Rob smile. "Al and me kinda took a likin ta him too," he told her. "He really helped us out a lot yest'rday. I 'on't know how we're gon' ev'r be able to thank 'im. But I'll think of somethin'. This is yor class." He said when they stopped.

"Oh. Thanks. Maybe I'll see you at lunch."

"I hope so," he said. His class is further away from Becky's than Alan's is from Michelle's. He had to do a soft sprint in order to get to class on time. He was almost there when he saw Mr. Jenson emerge around the corner. The last thing he needed was to give him an excuse to come down on him again, especially if he already knows his star quarterback is on vacation from playing right now. Immediately slowing to a fast pace walk he made it to class just before the bell rang.

Alan was just as diligent in keeping up with his schoolwork as Rob was. But whenever he wasn't swamped in homework, he spent his time with Michelle. The four of them would hang out at the pond on some Saturdays when the weather was nice enough. That wasn't often enough for Alan though cause Old Man Winter had already settled in for his ninety-day visit. There wasn't enough time created to spend with Michelle as far as he was concerned. They attended every extra-curricular school event together. The last one before school is out for Winter break is the Amory-Benson Christmas Ball. There weren't very many big events in the small town of Amory. The Christmas Ball gave the students a chance to dress up like royalty and feel like princes and princesses. It was the hype of the year for the students.

Sanderford helped sponsor this event as well. He believed that children should have a wide variety of experiences to ready them for the world they would walk into once life inside school was over. The more opportunity they had to socialize positively, the better. He made sure to find a few projects around the house for the boys to do so they could afford nice attire for the event.

It was a given that Alan and Michell would attend the ball together. But Becky was from a region where it was customary for a girl to be formally asked to such an event. Rob, thinking he and Becky had formed a special relationship by now, naturally assumed she would attend the event with him. It was Becky's desire to accompany Rob to the event, but a girl can't just forget everything she's been taught just because a handsome boy comes along and sweeps her grandpa off his feet.

At lunch, Michelle asked her what she was wearing to the ball. "I don't know," she told her.

"Whatta you mean you don't know? It's only two weeks away," Michelle reminded her.

"I don't think I'm going to the ball," Becky added.

"Why not?" Michelle asked her. "It's da biggest event of da year for us. Much bett'r than prom cause everybody gets to come. It's held at da City Pavilion, so we don't even have to be at school. And we get to dress up in pretty gowns like Cinderella. There'll be food, games, contests, dancing; da whole works. It's fun," she told her.

"It's sounds like a lotta fun," Becky agreed. "I know all about it. Grandpa is a sponsor."

"That's right. He is. So why ain't you comin'?" Michelle probed.

"I haven't been asked yet," Becky answered.

Michelle didn't understand that answer. She and Rob have been spending as much time together as her and Alan. Most times they all hung out together. She thought for sure they were a thing. She asked carefully in a confused kinda way, "I thought you and Rob w're 'it'?"

"Rob hasn't asked me yet," Becky replied. "I've been asked by plenty, but none of them is named Rob Barlow."

Rob and Alan heard the last of that conversation on the way to the table with their lunch tray. Rob sat down beside Becky. "I thought you w're my girl, Becky. Why do I have to ask you to go to da ball with me? I thought that was a given," he said to her.

"Where I'm from, the proper order is for the boy to ask and the girl to accept or refuse. If girls just assume, we're considered loose girls. I'm no loose girl Rob Barlow," she explained.

Rob hadn't been anywhere other than the four corners of the small town of Amory. He thought up to this point, that every place and everybody was the same. Becky taught him a new thing just now. He wondered what other kind of new things were beyond the invisible walls of Amory. "I'm sorry, Becky. I didn't know," he said first. "Will you be my steady girl?" he asked her. "And will you be my date to da Christmas Ball?"

"Rob," she said, "It took you long enough to ask. Yes, I will." She spoke all proper like.

Michelle then looked at Alan as if she expected him to follow suit behind Rob. "Yur from Amory," he said. "Y'all do thangs different h're." She slapped him across the shoulder playfully. "Besides, you already know yur my girl. And you already know I 'on't wanna go to da ball with nobody else but you."

Michelle didn't even think about arguing with that. "That's what I'm talkin' about," she said smiling.

#

This would be the first Amory-Benson Christmas Ball Rob has attended. Ethel had tried to get him to go in previous years, but he just wasn't interested. He wasn't interested in a lot of things before Alan and Becky came along. He didn't realize until now that life is more than community projects for the elderly. Life is good. And better with friends.

Needless to say, everything is new to Alan. Life has new meaning to him also since all of that homeless trestle rat business is behind him. He couldn't be happier. At least that's what he thought until he saw Michelle walk through the Pavilion doors. His smile illuminated the room. She looked exactly like he imagined a real-life Cinderella would look in her floor length white sequenced gown. Her hair was wrapped in a bun pinned to one side with a sequenced pin. When she entered the room, he couldn't seem to focus on anything else. Rob was on his own tonight. "Is Cinderella as pretty as you?" he asked her.

"You've nev'r read Cinderella," she asked him.

"No," he answered.

"Or seen da movie?"

"No," he said again.

"We're gon have to fix that," she told him.

Actually, Rob wasn't on his own. He was with the one person he wanted to be with when he wasn't with Alan. He became completely speechless, again, when he saw her. Apparently girls dressed different where she's from too. She was the only girl at the ball in a fitted gown, sparkling red with a sheer overlay that flowed softly as she walked towards him. "Hi Becky. You look great!"

"Rob Barlow. You're making me feel like a bowl of cereal. That's not what you say to a girl who went through as much effort as I did to get ready for this night." she schooled him.

She certainly didn't look like a bowl of cereal, Rob thought. He knew exactly what girls where she's from wanted to hear, "You look very pretty," he corrected.

It was a special night for the girls. They entreated their imaginations to live out a girlish fantasy. But it was a magical night for both Alan and Rob having never had this experience before. It would be a night they wouldn't soon forget.

§

Alan had entered a perfect realm of peace reminiscing on the love of his life. But his peace was interrupted when he suddenly yearned to hear her sweet voice. He was glad Rob and Chasidy had visited him. But now, his heart won't be content until she's by his side again. Her absence took him back in time once more when they spent nearly two weeks apart over the Christmas Holiday. It would have been the worst two weeks ever had it not been for his temporary parents and Rob.

§

Alan didn't see Michelle much over the winter holiday break. She lived further away than Becky and it was too cold to hang out by the pond. They were the longest two weeks of his life. Rob and Becky, however, spent lots of time together due to his association with Mr. Sanderford and them living right up the road from him.

Alan bought Michelle a gift for Christmas. He wanted to be certain she received it. It was already Christmas Eve, and he hadn't been able to connect with her yet. He called to ask her if he could come over. "I'll meet you somewhere instead," she suggested. "I have something for you too."

"Okay, where?" he asked her.

"Meet me in front of da drug store," she said. They walked from the drugstore to the café where they shared a large order of chili-cheese fries. Michelle liked seeing the town lit up in Christmas splendor, so from there they walked around town enjoying the scenery. They ended up in the park where they sat on a bench until it was too cold to stay any longer. "I guess I've made you wait long enough," he said to her smiling.

"I was wonderin' when you w're gonna get around ta this," she replied.

"How come you didn't ask me?" he asked.

"B'cause girls from Amory or nowhere else don't beg for gifts." They both laughed making a tease at Becky. "B'sides, I didn't want you runnin' off as soon as you gave it to me," she added. "I got to spend more time with ya this way."

"Yeah, I've missed you somethin' awful too. I didn't know a week could last so long," he told her. Then he reached inside his jacket pocket and pulled out a small gift bag. She ruffled through the paper to find a lovely silver bracelet with the engraving: Al heart Mic. He had it made special just for her. The shop owner adjusted the price so he could afford it because he knew he was the boy from the railroad trestle.

"Alan, this is beautiful. You must've spent all da money you had on this," she said.

Alan laughed. "Almost," he said. "But yur worth it. I like you a lot, Mic."

"Mic," she smiled, "I like that." Then she gave him the gift she got him. He smiled when he opened a box that held a locket on a chain with her picture in it. "Now you'll nev'r be alone again," she said, "cause I'll aways be with you." They shared a special Christmas Eve first love kiss and a slow walk towards home. They didn't even notice how the cold didn't bother them on the long walk back to the drugstore.

"Merry Christmas, Mic," he said.

"Merry Christmas, Al," she said back.

#

Rob was visiting Becky too. He made sure Mr. Sanderford had enough wood inside for the fireplace. Then he and Becky sat out on the back porch talking. Sanderford's house sat at the edge of a patch of trees. Becky commented on how cold they looked without leaves to keep them warm. Rob looked at her in astonishment, "I nev'r thought about it like that b'fore," he chuckled. Then he thought about her comment about boys and girls from her region. "So, do they have rules about what a boy should give a girl for Christmas where yur from?" he asked her.

She answered smiling, "Nothing about what to give. And only one about what not to give."

"Well, what's that one rule?" he asked.

"Don't give anything if your heart's not in it," she told him. He smiled and handed her a small box. She opened it excitedly but there was nothing in it. Looking at him in bewilderment, she said, "There's nothing here, Robert."

"I know," Rob said. "What w're you thinkin' would be in there?" he asked her.

"I don't know. I..." she stuttered.

"Becky, what did you wanna see when you opened da box? Really?" Rob pressed.

"A ring," she finally answered. "I wanted to see a ring. A promise to our future together."

Smiling, he said to her, "Yur da prettiest girl I know, Becky. I imagine yur da prettiest girl in da whole world."

"You're full of flattery, Robert. What else are you thinking?" Becky asked.

"Look in da box again," he told her." Then he took hold of her hand and touched the center of the box with her finger. "My heart is right h're. I can't ask you to marry me yet. We're only fourteen. But in two years, if you haven't run me off, I plan to do just that." She smiled back at him. Then he pulled a chain out of his pocket with a ring on it. He placed it around her neck. "Until then," he said.

"Until then, Robert," Becky agreed.

The boys made it in at about the same time. When they got home Ethel could hardly wait to ask them, "Did they like their gifts?"

"Rob!" Alan yelled at his friend.

"I didn't say anythin'!" Rob yelled back. "Ma Ethel knows everythin'."

Ethel chuckled softly. "Go bring in wood for da fire. Both of ya."

Ethel heard Rob ask him on the way out, "Well, did she?"

#

Sanderford and Becky were due over for Christmas dinner. Ethel was up early getting things ready for their guests. Rob and Al were allowed to sleep in. They would be plenty busy for the rest of the day once they did arise making sure the elderly was set for the cold weather headed their way.

Money was scarce but she made sure Christmas gifts for the boys wouldn't be the sacrifice. She wanted to make sure Alan's first Christmas with them was a memorable one. They were the only gifts under the tree. Ethel didn't mind not receiving a gift from them. She felt blessed just having her two wonderful boys. As long as they were healthy and happy, she would be content.

Alan and Rob didn't surface until close to ten-thirty. The girls had become their favorite conversation. They spent the night talking about Michelle and Becky and playing checkers. When they did surface, they dressed and made their way straight to Ethel to give her their gift. It was pricey for two young boys, but they put their monies together to get the nicest gift they could afford. "I thought you boys w're gonna sleep all day," she told them smiling. "Merry Christmas." She held her arms open for a Christmas hug. She squeezed them both as tight as she could, giving them both a sweet kiss on the head. They had gotten so tall, she had to make adjustments just for the kiss. "My, my," she said, "how much you've grown just since this summer. By New Year's Day, you'll be grown men." She spoke with a bit of melancholy in her voice. Rob noticed.

"You okay, Ma?" he asked her.

"I'm just fine, Baby," she said, "just fine." Rob motioned to Alan to give her the gift. He reached it to her without a word said. Only a smile. She sat down at the table to open the long narrow red box with a simple green ribbon on it. The tears she held back only moments ago made their appearance trickling down her face when she saw the beautiful triple heart pendant with a single diamond on each heart, hanging from a gold chain. "One for da three of us," she said.

Alan spoke, "It's real 14 karat gold. Rob and me put our money t'geth'r to get it for you."

"Yeah," Rob added. "We didn't wanna get you any of that fake stuff. You deserve da best." Ethel left the room in tears. She was gone for a long time. In fact, she didn't come back. When she regained her composure, she called the boys to her in the living room. She handed each of them a nice size box. They quickly opened them to find fancy hand-carved wooden boxes inside with designs of fish and worms and other things related to fishing. Alan squealed a joyous thank you to Ethel. "Fishing is my favorite thing to do," he said to her. "Thank you Ma." He didn't even say Ethel. Just Ma. Ethel thought that was even better than the gold necklace. The boys ran off grinning in opposite directions. Rob went to his bedroom while Alan went outside. When they both returned to the living room, they each had store bought fishing rods to give to each other. The three of them laughed from deep in their bellies at the perfect gifts they all had gotten each other.

But Alan had two more gifts to deliver. Before they started their community service, Alan wanted to see his temporary parents. Rob hadn't met them yet. This was a good time to change that. "Rob, I need to go across town," he said.

"For what?" Rob asked him.

"Come with me. I'll show you."

"What about da projects?" Rob asked him.

"I won't be long. I promise." Alan ran back outside to grab his gifts. Rob followed him. "Come on, let's go."

They walked hurriedly through town until they came to a big white two-story house with yellow shutters on it. Alan stopped in front of it. "Is this where yor temporary parents live?" Rob asked him.

"Yes."

"You left a house like this to stay und'r a railroad track?"

Alan just stared at Rob for a moment. "Come on," he then said just before knocking. When Mrs. Marshall opened the door, her smile met with his and she grabbed him pulling him close to her for a long overdue hug. "Hi Ma Kelly. Merry Christmas."

Mr. Marshall heard Alan's voice and joined them at the door. "Son!" he said. "We didn't think we would get to see you this Christmas," he said as he joined in the hug.

"I wouldn't let Christmas pass without seein' you," Al confessed. "I've missed you."

"We've missed you too, Son." Rob watched them carefully. He could see they cared a lot about each other. He was even more confused than ever as to why Alan would leave them.

Once inside, Alan turned to Rob to introduce him. "This is the boy I told you about. His name is Rob."

"Hello Rob," they both said. But then not anything else for a few seconds. They were collecting their feelings, trying to figure out how they felt about the boy who took Alan away from them. "It's nice to meet you, Rob," Mr. Marshall finally said.

"Yes. We've often wondered about the boy Alan was so infatuated with that he had to leave us. Come warm your hands. I'll fix you some hot cocoa," Mrs. Marshall added.

"We can't stay," Alan said. "I just wanted to bring you these." He handed them their gifts.

They hurriedly received them, and Mrs. Marshall dashed off to get Alan's presents. "We didn't know if we would see you today. But we were hoping. Merry Christmas, Son." She looked at him with pleading eyes. "Are you sure you can't stay ... just long enough for one cup of cocoa?"

Rob could see how much they wanted to spend time with him. But more important than that, he could see how much Alan wanted to stay too. "We have ta gath'r firewood for da community," Alan explained, "b'fore it gets too cold outside."

"That's nice of you. I think. Is this a community service job?" Mrs. Marshall asked disappointedly.

The boys didn't know what that meant exactly. They understood better when Mr. Marshall asked, "You boys been in trouble with da law?"

"No, Sir. Nothin' like that. Rob's Ma Ethel helps out in da community. Rob helps her and I help him," Alan explained. They were glad to hear that, but still disappointed he couldn't stay.

Rob couldn't stand it any longer. "Al, why don't you stay h're and visit with 'em. I can get da firewood on my own."

"It'll take all day by yorself," Alan warned.

"Just enough time for you to spend with yor family. It's Christmas. You haven't seen 'em since you left," Rob explained. "I can see you wanna stay as much as they want cha to. Meet me at da pond at four o'clock. That'll give us time to get home for dinn'r."

"You sure about this?" Alan asked.

All Rob could think about at that moment is Alan leaving a beautiful family and home like this to stay under a railroad trestle just to be close to him. A sacrifice such as that deserved a sacrifice in return. "As sure as you w're da day you left these good people." Then he spoke to Alan's temporary parents. "Mr. and Mrs. Marshall, Alan told me how much he likes you and that you w're good to 'im. He hated hurtin' you da way he did. Now that I've met you, it kinda put a damp'r in my spirit too. Alan's gon come back to visit y'all more often. I'm gonna see ta that. Merry Christmas y'all."

6

GROWN UP LOVE

It was becoming the norm at school seeing the four of them together, Alan and Michelle and Rob and Becky. So much so that their names sort of flowed together. The routine stayed the same throughout the summer months. The four of them had become inseparable. Their high school infatuations had blossomed into full blown first loves.

They met down by the pond most days after Alan and Rob had finished working. When Alan introduced Michelle to his favorite thing to do and tried teaching her how to fish; he soon learned that she isn't the sportsman type. He reached her the fishing pole, at which point she looked at him cross-eyed and asked, "What am I gon do with that?" pitching her high-pitch twang even higher.

"Catch fish," he answered.

"Why would I wanna do that?"

"Don't you eat fish?"

"Not from out h're," she clarified. "From da supermarket."

Alan laughed. "Well, where do ya think da supermarket get 'em from?"

"I don't know," Michelle answered. "But if you tell me they come outta this nasty water I'm not eatin' anoth'r bite ev'r." Alan laughed even more. Rob and Becky joined him.

Rob hoped he'd have better luck with Becky. But before he could ask, she grabbed his fishing rod and asked, "Whatta you using for bait? I don't see any crickets."

"Crickets!" Michelle squealed. "Whatta you gon do with crickets?"

"We use night crawlers," Rob told Becky.

"Whatta night crawlers?" Michelle asked still in disgust.

Rob opened a box and pulled out a fat juicy worm and held it up so the girls could see it. Becky held out her hand for it. Michelle decided she had learned enough about fishing for, well, a lifetime. She found a soft spot to sit in the shade far away from the water and the worms. "I'll be right ov'r h're when y'all are done," she told Alan.

Rob helped Becky bait her hook with the worm. He was highly impressed with her sportsmanship. He just had to rub it in Alan's face. They wouldn't be true friends if he didn't. "Looks like yur gonna have to find a new favorite thing to do if you wanna hang out with Mic," he said grinning.

"Yea," Becky added, "she loves da café."

"Y'all got jokes," Alan replied. "I'll be back." He went over to where Michelle was sitting under the tree. "You gon make me pull my locket out?" he asked her. "I'd rath'r have da real you sittin' next to me."

"I'm sorry," Michelle said, "I'm just not da outdoorsy type. I wish I could be more like Becky sometimes. She and Rob are perfect t'geth'r."

He sat down close to her. Then he reached behind her to pull her scrunchie off of her hair. "Yur awful pretty Mic." When he loosened her hair, he fixed it around her face. "You and me are perfect t'geth'r too. But if yur gonna act like a Ms Prissy girl, you should wear yor hair like one," he said. "There."

"You happy now?" Michelle asked.

"I've been happy all along," He answered. Then he said, "Don't ev'r wish yur somebody else. Becky can't hold a can of worms to you," he teased. "If you nev'r learn how to fish, it won't make a bit-a difference to me. But I would like to have my girl next to me though." He stood up reaching for her hand to help her up. She decided to join him. They found a shady spot by the pond where they could sit and talk while he fished. On their way there he gave Rob and Becky a special grin that boasted; 'all jokes are on y'all'.

The sun was starting to set. They had to get the girls home. They all walked Michelle home first since she stayed further away. As far as she would let them, that is. Rob walked Becky home alone. But every chance they got; they met up together. Sometimes by the pond, sometimes at the café. Sometimes at Mr. Sanderford's house, sometimes at Ma Ethel's and even sometimes at Alan's temporary parents' home.

But the one place they never met was at Michelle's home. They often wondered why. But no one ever asked her. They trusted that she would tell them when she was ready.

Each day they met, Alan and Rob had a small treat for the girls: a flower they picked from the side of the road, plums, peaches, or apples they grabbed from a neighbor's tree. They even brought store bought candy once or twice as a special treat.

The girls weren't above spoiling them too. They collaborated in preparing picnic lunches that they shared underneath the tree by the pond. The same tree Alan fell from when he first met Rob. Rob shared that story with them one day during one of their picnics.

The next two years were two of the best years ever for Alan and Rob as they grew closer to the girls. Alan thought more and more about marrying Michelle. He even spoke to Papa Stan about it. "Marriage is a big step," Stan told him. "Much too big for you to be thinking about at your age."

"How old were you when you and Ma Kelly married?"

"Those were different times," Stan answered, not really answering his question.

Alan waited for him to continue. When he didn't, he asked again. "Well. How old?"

Stan thought about him and his wife and the mistake they made when they were young. He called Kelly to include her in the conversation. Before they told him their story, Kelly asked him, "Are you and Mic trying to cover up somethin'? Is that why you wanna marry her?"

At first Alan was clueless as to what they meant. But after thinking about it, he blurted out, "No! No.

Mic is fine. I just know that I love 'er and I wanna spend the rest of my life with 'er. I've known that since before we actually met." He declared definitely.

The Marshalls were glad to hear it. They shared with him anyway their story of the mistake they made and how it cost them the ability to have children of their own. "That's why when you happened along, we thought our prayers had been answered and you would become our son," Mr. Marshall said.

Alan more than understood now. You don't have to be blood related to be family. "I am yor son if you'll still have me," he said.

"We'd love to have ya, Sweetheart," Mrs. Marshall said.

It was Rob, however, who had a promise to keep. And he was more than anxious to keep it. Promptly on his sixteenth birthday, he made ready to make good on that promise. He rose early on the morning of July 10th. Ethel wondered what was going on in that meticulous mind of his. She knew it was serious. He walked around her in circles until he could find the nerves to talk to her. "You need help with breakfast, Ma?" he asked her.

"If you've a mind to. Thank you. I haven't started yet, though. You boys aren't usually up this early on a Saturday," she said. "I was just havin' my coffee. Sit. Tell me what's got you up so early."

He hesitated for just a second or two. Then he asked her, "Do you know what day this is, Ma?"

"Absolutely," she answered. "It's Saturday just like I said before," she teased. "Oh, by da way, Happy Birthday."

"I knew you knew what day it is," he said smiling.

"I've been so busy; I haven't had time to get yor gift. I'll run out and do that taday though," she told him.

"You don't have to do that. I don't need a gift," he said. "I do need yor help though."

"With what Dear?"

"I wanna marry Becky," he blurted out. "How do I do that?"

"Sixteen is a bit young ta be thinkin' about marriage, isn't it?" she asked him.

"No Mam," he answered, "not when yur as sure as I am." He paused looking Ethel straight face to face, in the eyes. "Two years ago, for Christmas, I gave Becky a promise ring b'cause I was too young to propose to 'er then. But I promised 'er that when I was sixteen and if she hadn't run me off, I would ask her to marry me."

Ethel remembered a conversation she and Sanderford had the first year Rob and Becky met about this very subject. *'He's gonna be tickled silly ta know that he was right.'* She thought. She was glad Rob came to her for help with this. "Okay. Da proper thing to do is ask her grandfather's permission first. Then you can see what Becky has to say. She might have changed her mind by now. Two years is a long time," Ethel told him.

"She hasn't," he replied. "She still wears my ring around 'er neck. Sometimes, when she doesn't know I'm watchin', I see 'er playin' with it. Tryin' it on. Makin' sure it still fits."

That made Ethel smile. "Well, if yur sure about this ..."

"I am," he interrupted her.

"Why don't I ask Whit and Becky ov'r for dinn'r this eve'nin' so da two of ya can talk," she finished what she started earlier.

"Thanks Ma."

Ethel didn't mention the short conversation she and Sanderford had about them two years ago, although she was tempted. He was nervous bringing up the subject to her. She was curious to see how he would conduct himself in front of Sanderford.

After breakfast, once the boys were out of the house, she called Sanderford to invite him and Becky over for dinner with a hint of what to expect. "Wear somethin' oth'r than dem ol' coveralls, Whit. This is Robert's birthday," she said.

"It is!" Sanderford said excitedly. "Becky and I will pick up a gift for 'im sometime taday."

"This ain't no birthday party though," Ethel said. "And he don't want no store-bought gifts. He made it clear, there's only one gift he's interested in."

"What's that?" Sanderford asked.

"R'member those weddin' bells you heard a couple years back?" she asked him.

Sanderford immediately began to laugh. "Yes, I do. I knew that was comin'. It's getting' so that every time ya see one ya see da other. I'll pick up somethin' for 'im anyway, so he won't know we had this conversation," Sanderford said.

"Great. Be h're around 5:30." Ethel instructed.

Ethel coached Rob as much as she could on the matter while they awaited their arrival. She's been single all of her days, so she wasn't really sure of the specifics. But she made a suggestion that made sense to him. "We'll have dinner at 5:30. I know yur anxious but wait until dinn'r is ov'r before talkin' with 'im. For some reason a man's more accommodatin' on a full belly." Rob smiled at that.

"Ma, whatta think he'll say? Will he say we're too young?" he asked.

"Whatta you think?" Alan asked in a slightly higher pitch. "Da way he's always makin' boast about you, it's a wonder he ain't asked 'er for ya." Rob grinned even harder at that.

"Yea, he does like me a little," he agreed. "But he likes you too," he added. "But then, you ain't tryin' ta marry his granddaught'r."

There was a knock. Ethel stood to answer with one last comforting comment to Rob. "Alan's right. Chin up like a man. You'll be fine." Then she kissed him on the forehead like she did when he was younger.

Alan in his usual playful manner whispered to Rob grinning his Chester cat grin, "Rob, whatta you gon do if he says you can't marry 'er though?"

"Shut up," Rob responded.

"Happy birthday, Son," Sanderford said handing him a gift. It's from me and Becky both. She picked it out for ya."

"Thank you, Sir. In that case, I'm sure I'll love it," Rob told him. "Hi Becky," he then said.

"Hi Robert. Happy birthday."

"Thanks."

"Robert, why don't you get Sanderford somethin' to wet his throat with while I set da table."

"Okay, Ma."

"I'll help you, Ma Ethel," Becky said.

"So how old are you taday?" Sanderford asked knowing already his age.

"Sixteen," Rob answered.

"Sixteen," Sanderford repeated. "I can r'member when you w're no tall'r than that chair leg there.

Getting' inta all kinds of mischief." Sanderford reminisced. "But you've grown into a fine young man. Yur gonna make some young gal a fine husband someday," he playfully taunted Rob, trying to calm him down a bit. Only Rob didn't know that.

Alan sat across from Rob with a continual goofy grin plastered to his face. Rob tried to ignore him. He was relieved when Ethel finally came in and announced that dinner was ready.

The small talk continued throughout dinner. Mostly between Ethel and Sanderford. Rob's belly was so full of butterflies, it's a wonder he could eat anything. He mostly smiled at Becky and tried diligently to ignore Alan. Becky noticed Alan making tease of Rob on the sly also. If it were any other day for any other reason, she would have come to Rob's rescue. But she too was a nervous wreck inside.

She couldn't imagine why the procrastination, but it was sheer torture to her. She just wanted it all to be over. Sanderford sat back in his chair rubbing his slightly enlarged belly. "Ethel, that was a fine meal," he told her.

"Thank you Whit. I'm glad you enjoyed it," she said winking at Rob. "Would you care for anythin' else?" she asked him.

"Not a thing. I can't eat anoth'r bite."

"What about you, Becky," Ethel asked. "More desert?"

"No thank you. Would ya like me to help you with the dishes?"

"Oh, you can help me clear da table. I can get those after you leave. Let's go visit in da livin' room for a spell."

Ethel wanted to be in near proximity in case Rob needed a little support. He may be developing into a fine young man, but he's still her baby as far as she's concerned. The conversation was just beginning when she and Becky entered from the kitchen. Rob was fidgety and nervous. He had known Mr. Sanderford all his life. And yet at this very moment, it felt like he was talking to a complete stranger. Sanderford decided he'd help him out a little. "You okay, Son? Looks like you got somethin' on yor mind."

"I do Sir," Rob answered. He thought briefly about the Christmas promise he had made to Becky. He had no idea it would be this difficult keeping that promise. He knew Mr. Sanderford liked him. But liking a guy is one thing and letting him marry his granddaughter is a whole new ball game. None-the-less, he couldn't break his promise to Becky. He didn't even want to. "Mr. Sanderford, I wanna marry Becky. Ma Ethel says I need yor permission b'fore that can hap'en," he finally blurted out.

"You just turned sixteen, Son. Isn't that a little young for marryin," Sanderford asked.

"Yes sir," Rob answered. "We won't be gettin' married this early. But I promised Becky two Christmases ago that I would give her an engagement ring when I turned sixteen. I don't wanna break my promise to 'er. Ma Ethel says a man's word outta be his bond," he explained. Suddenly Alan was no longer grinning at his friend. He could see how nervous he was and actually empathized with him. He was hoping this whole thing was over for him already and he and Becky could get back to being Rob and Becky.

Mr. Sanderford was proud of the young man Rob was growing up to be. A young man he already thought of as his grandson. He was impressed with

Rob's answer. He couldn't let him know just how happy he is just yet thought. It's customary to make a perspective groom work for his bride. "Whatta yor plans for da future? How will you take care of my granddaught'r?"

"I ain't afraid of work, Mr. Sanderford," he answered. "You've seen that for yorself. I'll make sure Becky's taken care of." Rob's voice has become stronger, bolder; speaking with much more confidence than when he first started.

By now, Becky and Ethel have found themselves a seat on the sofa. "Rebecca," Sanderford spoke, "how do you feel about all of this? Marryin' this young man, I mean."

"Grandpa, if I traveled the world over, I wouldn't find a finer man than Robert anywhere," she answered looking her grandpa straight faced in the eyes. Ethel fully agreed with Becky, but it wasn't her place to say so right now, so she just sat quietly smiling.

"Ethel, your Rob asked permission to marry my Becky just before you girls came in. "Whatta you think about that?" he asked Ethel.

"Whit, if you and I traveled da world ov'r, we wouldn't find a finer couple. Aside from Alan and Mic that is," she added. "But not until aft'r their schoolin' is done."

"I agree whole-heartedly, Ethel," Sanderford said. "You kids have our blessings. When school is ov'r. That's just enough time to plan da biggest, fanciest weddin' ev'r in da history of Amory for my only granddaught'r and a young man I already think of as family."

"Congratulations you too!" Ethel told them. Even Alan was grinning again. This time with his friend.

7

REALITY CHECK

§

Neither Michelle nor AJ had seen Alan since the accident. They were both worried about him. Unfortunately, Little Guy had no choice but to wait. Children weren't allowed in ICU and his release was already being processed. He was scheduled to go back to the hotel with Rob the next day. Chasidy let Rob explain Al's condition. She knew he wanted to be the one to do it. She peeped in briefly on the babies and Caitlin after which they all joined them in Mic's room. Chasidy made it a mission to convince Michelle to strap on her big girl bras and go see about her husband. "Rob explained about Al well enough?" Chasidy asked.

"Yes. Rob says he's all bandaged up. But he believes he's gonna be alright because of his interactions with y'all. I don't know if I can handle that," she explained. "But I'm b'lieving' with y'all. I have to. I don't my husband any oth'r way." Michelle talked as she played with little Remi.

"You may need to get to know 'im differently," Chasidy said to her.

"Whatta you mean?"

"Yor husband needs you. Yur da otha half of his strength. Just like he's da otha half of yors. You need to be in that room with him, Mic. He needs to hear yor voice, feel yor touch, smell yor perfume. Every one of his senses needs to absorb you. So, all that fear yur harboran' right h're," she touched her heart, "needs to be channeled inta yor strength so you can get betta and go see about yor husband."

"I just don't if I can handle seein' 'im this way," she said again. Michelle began to sound weak.

"Do you know why Alan jokes so much about da bad things that hap'ans in his life?" Chasidy asked her.

"No, why?"

"B'cause he refuses to let da bad things ovar take 'im. It's his way of stayin' positive. Keepin hope alive. If da tables w're turned, where would Al be?" Chasidy asked her.

"Right there beside me," she answered.

"You once said that Al is only serious during football season. FYI girl. He's serious about you and AJ all da time. It wasn't until after I told him how worried you w're that he squeezed my hand."

"That's nothin' but da truth," Barlow finally spoke. "His whole world evolves around da two of you."

Michelle knew what she needed to do. Her dear friend was right. She had to stop being a Ms Prissy Wimpy Girl and go be with her husband. When the nurse came in to administer her meds, she refused them. "I don't want them. They make me sleep too much. I need to see my husband. He needs me. I can't be with him if I'm asleep all day," she told them.

The next day, just before taking AJ to the hotel, Rob took her to visit her husband. When she first entered the room, she hurried back out in tears. She allowed herself to cry until she couldn't shed any more tears. Then she went back in leaving the wimpy girl outside. She showered him with kisses and stayed with him the whole day, holding his hand, and talking to him.

Alan basked at her sweet voice and the faint scent of her lovely perfume. The same one she's worn for as long as he's known her. The universe is finally co-operating with him. Now if he could only see her beautiful face, all would be right in the universe. For now, he had to be content with seeing her in his head. To him, she is still as pretty today as she ever was...

§

The small town of Amory was all abuzz about the engagement of the sixteen-year-olds. Neither Ethel nor Sanderford kept it a secret. They were proud of their young people and couldn't wait to see them as husband and wife. Some were ecstatic for Ethel and Sanderford. Others were sure they were covering up to protect Becky's honor. But when they found out the marriage wouldn't take place until after they graduated high school, they didn't quite know what to make of an engagement between two people so young. It was as if they just didn't understand love at first sight and at such a young age. At school they were known as 'The Couple'.

The weekend after the nerve pounding proposal dinner, the two couples met at the café. Supposedly working on homework assignments, they were doing more laughing and kidding around than anything else. Michelle's mother came into the café to get lunch for herself and Mr. Peterson. She watched her daughter for more than a few minutes interacting with people she had never seen before. She looked extremely happy. Happier than she had ever seen her with her old friends. She noticed there was no food on the table though. She asked the waitress, "That young group over there, have they ordered yet?"

"Yeah, they got an order of chili cheese fries to share between them. They're in here all the time. Order the same thing most times. I don't think they have any money. But they do enjoy each other's company though," the waitress told her.

Mrs. Peterson made a deal with the manager to get them whatever they wanted from now on and she would take care of the bill for them. She told the waitress, "After I leave, go take their order. Make sure they get whatever they want." She tipped her twenty dollars. "Do that every time they come in here and you'll get one of these."

"Thanks! I will."

#

Becky surrounded herself with magazines about weddings and things associated with them. She and Mic talked about it every chance they got for the next three months. Michelle was becoming just as excited as Becky is. Becky had already asked Mic to be her maid of honor, but then she had another brilliant thought. They were hanging out at the café one day just before dust getting ready to walk Michelle home. Before leaving the table, Becky took a mental picture of the four of them sitting there. Rob noticed. "Whatcha thinkin' on Becky?" he asked her.

"Ever since I've been here, we four have been doing everything together," she answered.

"Yeah, so," Rob said.

Becky looked a definite look at Alan and then at Michelle. "What?" they both said simultaneously.

"So, if y'all get engaged too, we could have a double wedding and really throw this little town for a loop," Becky said. Nobody saw that coming. They all sat staring back at Becky like she was trapped in another dimension, and they were trying to figure out how to bring her back. She knew the guys were turning pages together, but she was sure the thought must have crossed Mic's mind at least once or twice. "Seriously, Mic. Don't you think that's a great idea?"

"It's a great idea but where I'm from, a girl don't get engaged unless someone asks ta marry her," Michelle answered. Rob, Becky, and Michelle immediately looked at Alan who didn't say anything. Then Michelle said, "It's getting' late. I gotta get home."

Alan stood to walk her home. "You want us to wait on ya?" Rob asked Alan before he left.

"Naw, I'm good," Alan said. "I'll see ya at home."

#

On the walk home, Alan was quiet as he held Michelle's hand. He was thirteen years old when he first thought of marrying the prettiest girl in school. Rob told him he would never get her to turn him a look. He had done that and more. He'd gotten her to fall in love with him. *'So why haven't I asked her to marry me?'* He thought to himself. *'Is it because of what Ma Kelly and Papa Stan said?'* He was lost in that thought when Michelle spoke.

"If it bothers you that much, Al..." Michelle started but stopped. "I'm sure Becky was just playin' around anyway."

Alan looked at Michelle smiling. "You would really marry me?" he asked, "a homeless kid with no family and no background, who lived under a railroad trussell for nearly three months."

"You won't know until you ask me," Michelle answered.

Alan stopped walking. He held both of her hands looking her in the eyes. "I have every intent to ask you to be my wife. But not like this on a walk with no ring ta show for it. Meet me at da café aft'r school t'morrow," he told her.

"Yur gonna have a ring by then?" she asked.

"Mic," he said, "I've had yor ring since b'fore Rob proposed ta Becky."

"So why haven't you asked me?"

"I've been lookin' all ov'r town for my nerves. I just caught up with 'em though." He kissed her softly. "Let's get you home b'fore yor dad sends da hounds out for ya."

"For da record," Michelle said, "Da Marshalls, Rob and Ma Ethel are family enough if you ask me." She corrected him on not having any family.

#

Michelle stepped into the house from a loving bliss into a living hell. Her dad had been waiting for her to get home. She could tell he wasn't happy. Her mom was clearly upset about something. "Dad what is it? I'm not late," she began to defend herself. "It's not even dark yet."

Mr. Peterson had run into Junior Green earlier today when he was slapped in the face with what he considered an ugly reality. He had thought all this time that Michelle was spending her time with Junior. He learned today that she wasn't. "Where've you been all eve'nin'?" he asked angrily.

"At da café. Doin' my homework with my friends." She answered.

"What friends?" Michelle looked at her mom who had been crying. "It's my understandin' you haven't hung out with yor friends for ov'r two years. So, who exactly have you been spendin' yor time with?"

"I've made new friends," Michelle said.

"Why haven't we met these new friends of yors? Is something wrong with 'em? Like maybe they live under a railroad track?" He literally yelled at Michelle like she was some kind of criminal. She had never seen her dad so angry. "You deliberately lied to us. Are those the kind of friends you want, the kind that make you lie to yor parents?"

"Dad, I didn't lie to you. I nev'r said who I was hangin' out with," Michelle explained.

"No, you didn't," her dad said. "That's exactly my point. What hap'ened ta you and Junior? Don't tell me you let that trussell rat run 'im off?"

As many times as she's heard Alan being called a trestle rat, it's never hurt as much as it did at that moment. "Alan's not a trussell rat! Did you get that from Junior Dad?" she yelled back at her dad.

"Don't you raise yor voice ta me, Michy!" Michelle looked at her mom again for help.

"Jeffrey, that's not called for," she tried to help. "I don't see anything wrong with da boy."

"You stay outta this, Val! And when you do speak, you say what I tell you to say!" He turned his attention back to Michelle. "Do you know how embarrassed I was to find out my daught'r has been hangin' out with dirt. Da whole town knew except me!" Michelle started to cry. She knew her dad would disapprove of her seeing Alan. But she didn't know he would be down-right hateful towards him.

"Dirt!"

"I hate to do this Michy. But you haven't left me much choice."

"Whatta you talkin' about? Whatta you gonna do?" she asked him.

"I'm pullin' you outta that school away from that boy."

"Dad, please, you can't do that!" Michelle pleaded.

"I can and I have. I've already spoken ta da director of Whispering Hills. That's where you'll be startin' immediately."

"Whispering Hills. That's not even in Amory. Yur sendin' me away from Mom?"

"It's for yor own good," He reasoned.

"How can being away from my mom be good for me? I won't go," Michelle protested. "I'm staying h're with Alan and Mom. You can't make me leave."

"If you don't go, I'll see to it that that boy nev'r lives a single day of his adult life as a free man. If I can't find a reason to have im put away, I'll conjure up one. You don't call 'im. You don't write 'im. You don't ask about 'im. If I feel like yur even thinkin' about 'im, it's only gonna mean trouble for 'im. You understand what I'm sayin' girl?" Michelle ran to her room slamming the door behind her. Her mother ran after her. "Val, you get back here! You leave her be!"

"Jeffrey, after you carry a child for nine months and give birth to it, then you can tell me what I can and can't do with my daught'r." Valerie was just as hurt by her husband's words as Michelle. If she couldn't understand the reason for his harshness, she knew Michelle couldn't either.

As soon as she sat down on the bed, Michelle fell into her mother's arms. She held her daughter for a long time. "Why does he hate Alan so, Mom? I don't understand. He doesn't even know 'im."

"I don't know, Baby. I don't understand it eith'r."

"If he makes me leave, I'll nev'r forgive 'im." Michelle told her mom.

"Is this boy worth losin' yor father ov'r?" her mother asked her.

"Is his hatred for 'im worth losin' me ov'r?" Michelle responded.

Mrs. Peterson lifted her daughter's head to look her in the face. "I can see yur in love with him." Michelle smiled. "So why haven't you brought 'im around ta meet us?"

"Because I knew Dad wouldn't like 'im. Al isn't rude and insensitive like Junior. And he isn't a star football player. He's just plain ol Al. I didn't think Dad would be so cruel though. Kids at school have been treating 'im that way since he started. Alan's a wonderful person. I don't like watchin' him being treated that way. And now by my own dad," Michelle explained.

"You do know yor father, don't you?"

"He wants to marry me, Mom. He was gonna propose ta me t'morrow," Michelle told her mom. "He said he's had my ring for months. But he couldn't find his nerves." They chuckled. "He's gonna wond'r what hap'ened ta me if I don't show up for school t'morrow. And da café." She looked at her mother with pleading eyes again. "Can't you talk to 'im? Make him understand." Michelle pulled out a picture of Al from her purse. She showed it to her mom.

"Well. He's downright handsome, Michy." They shared a smile in the mist of their tears. Her mom started slowly shaking her head. "This picture doesn't do 'im justice though." Her mom added.

"What?" Michelle asked surprised. "You've seen 'im in person?"

"Yes, I saw da four of you t'gether one Saturday at da cafe. You w're havin' so much fun."

"Why didn't you say somethin'? I would have loved for you to meet them."

"I was waitin' for you to make that move."

"I'm sorry. Now you won't get da chance to meet em, will you?"

"Unfortunately, there's no talkin' any sense into yor father when he's acting like this. We just have to wait 'im out Sweetheart."

Becky and Rob are getting married when they finish school. Becky wanted us to have a double weddin'. I liked that idea. That's why Alan was gonna propose t'morrow. So, we could get married togeth'r."

"How w're you gonna get yor dad to agree ta that?" "Maybe if he hadn't run up on Junior first. We might've had a chance." Michelle dropped her head. She didn't have any answers. She didn't want to leave her mom either.

"But Mom, Whispering Hills? I don't even think black kids go there."

"You'll be alright, Baby."

"But I'll miss you. And what if Alan..." she couldn't even say the words.

But her mom knew. "If Alan loves you, he'll wait for you. And as for me. Yur gonna get tired of seein' yor old mom poppin' in on ya. Yur still my baby, even as da beautiful young lady you've come to be."

#

The next day, Alan looked for Michelle all day at school. By lunchtime he was ready to go on a city-wide missing person's hunt. Especially when she wasn't at the table with Becky like she usually is when he and Rob arrives. "Have you seen 'er at all taday?" he asked Becky.

"No." Becky said. "There's been whispering all day though. But nobody's sharing with me."

"Me neith'r," Rob said. "And Junior is just a little too happy taday for some reason."

Alan was a nervous wreck. An entire week had passed but there was no Mic to be found. He didn't know exactly where Michelle lived. She never let him walk her all the way to her house. But he knew the neighborhood. He knocked on every door until he found the right one. He had knocked on so many doors, his knuckles hurt and had begun to swell. Finally, her father opened the door. "Hello Sir. My name's Al. Yor neighbor said this is where Mic lives. I was wonderin' if she's alright," he spoke nervously.

"Mic? If you mean Michelle, she's just fine," her father spoke rudely.

"But she hasn't been ta school all week," Alan said.

"That's none of yor concern. But since yur h're, you should know Michelle won't be comin' back to that school. If I had known she'd been hangin' out with you these past two years, I would've had a r'strainin ord'r put against ya. You can fa'get about seein' my daught'r. That's not gonna hap'en ev'r again. Now you go on away from h're. You got no bus'ness h're anymore. Go back to that trussell where you belong. All of ya!" he yelled at the three of them.

"What have you done?" Al asked him. "Where is she?"

"I don't have to answer to you. If you're not gone by da time I reach da phone, I'm calling da police!"

Alan turned and ran as fast as he could. Rob wanted to run after him, but he didn't want to leave Becky behind. "Go! I can keep up," she said.

But neither of them could catch up to Al. Rob knew where he was going though. When they got to the trestle, he was throwing rocks everywhere and screaming, "Son of Sam! That mean old Son of Sam! He took 'er away! He took Mic away from me!"

"Stay back, Becky!" Rob warned. "Al stop! Stop it! B'fore you hurt somebody!"

"I didn't tell ya ta follow me!" Alan spoke angrily.

"Then stop b'fore you hurt yorself!" Rob pleaded. "Al, please," he spoke more calmly.

Alan calmed himself. He was tired and out of breath. "I don't know what I was thinkin'. I was nev'r good enough for 'er. Everybody could see that except me. They're all right. I am just a trussell rat." He said in defeat.

"Everybody didn't call you a trussell rat," Rob said. "I nev'r did. I'll bet Mic nev'r did eith'r."

"Al Ferguson, there isn't a rat alive with eyes as handsome as yours. Mic thinks so too," Becky said.

"See Rob, she does think I'm a trussell rat," Alan said. "That's probably why she nev'r let me visit 'er at home."

"No, she doesn't, silly. She thinks you're handsome." Becky told him. "He has da handsomest amber eyes I've ever seen. She said to me all the time."

"Mic nev'r took any of us to 'er house. I'll bet that had more to do with 'er dad than us," Rob told him.

"Well, it makes no matt'r now. I'll nev'r see 'er again." Al said. "Why would he do this, Rob? Why would he take 'er away from me. I would nev'r hurt Mic."

"I know that Al," Rob told him. "Ma Ethel says we can drive ourselves crazy tryin' ta figure oth'r folks out."

Alan reached into his pocket and pulled out the ring. "I've had this since before you and Becky got engaged. We w're gonna meet at da café a week ago so I could ask 'er prop'r to marry me. I guess I won't be needin' it anymore." He dropped it in the rocks. Rob picked it up.

"Mic's comin' back," he said, "and when she does, she won't stop until she finds 'er way to you."

"How do you know?" Alan asked.

"B'cause I've seen da two of ya t'gether. R'member? When she's with you, she's right where she wants to be."

Alan pondered that thought for a moment. Then he gave himself a real reality check. "Yur right," he agreed. "We're still kids by legal right. She has to do what 'er dad tells her to do. But we won't be kids always." He reached for the ring back. "Thanks. I'll hang on ta this for a while," he concluded.

"We'd bett'r get home, Al. Ma Ethel will be worried," Rob said. "And we've gotta get Becky home first."

"You two go ahead. I'm where I b'long," Alan told them.

"Oh well," Becky said, "I guess we're staying too."

Alan argued, "What? You can't stay out h're. This ain't no place for a girl."

"Well, Rob isn't leaving you here alone. And I'm not walking home by myself," Becky reasoned. "Besides. This ain't no place for nobody."

Alan looked at Rob. Rob took a seat under the trestle. Becky followed him, taking a seat beside him. Alan followed Becky, but he didn't sit. "Come on guys," Alan said, "b'fore Mr. Sanderford come lookin' for us." Then he said, "Well, for you two," almost smiling.

Alan put on a good face after that. But those closest to him knew he wasn't the same. His Chester Cat grin was just a regular old grin now and didn't luminate the room like it did before. The good thing that came from this is that he found himself spending more time with his temporary parents since he felt like a third wheel with Rob and Becky.

#

It's been two years. Rob and Becky were married right after high school. Sanderford had given Becky a wedding of dreams. It too became the talk of the small town. It was a bittersweet moment for Alan. He and Mic were supposed to be with them.

Mrs. Peterson kept a watch on Alan from a distance to see how he was faring. He looked sad most times. But if not sad, certainly not like he looked the day she saw him at the café with Michelle. On occasion she would see pretty girls flirting with him. But he didn't seem to notice them. She felt bad for him. As bad as she felt for her daughter. On occasion she would try to reason with Mr. Peterson concerning their daughter and Alan, but he was as stubborn as a mule when it came to Alan. She just didn't understand it. He seemed to be such a nice young man.

Shortly after, Rob enlisted in the Army to serve his country. Alan tried to follow suit, but he was unable to. The Army couldn't find enough definitive information on him. His heart was broken when Rob left him also. "I'm not even good enough to serve my country," he complained to Rob. "And now yur leavin' me, too."

"I'll never leave you Al. Don't make this harder than it has to be. I'm gonna miss you too. But at least this way I know I have someone h're to watch ov'r Ma Ethel and Becky 'til I get back," Rob said. "That's more important than fightin' for yor country. Ta me anyway. And I'll be back, Al, ta all three of ya."

Rob was gone for just over two years. With no Rob and no Michelle, it was the worst two years of Alan's life. He and Rob hadn't been separated for more than a night's sleep since they met eight years ago at the age of twelve and thirteen. And he was still dealing with Michelle missing in action. But he made the best of it. He was glad he had stayed in touch with his temporary parents. They were a big help during these times. He went on to college to continue his education in carpentry beginning his journey as a civil engineer. He kept himself busy with school and work until Rob got back. Rob's term was abruptly shortened when he fell from a scaffold and injured his back. Uncle Sam could no longer use him, so they sent him home to heal.

Becky took a leave of absence from her job to care for her husband. Ethel was pleased with that. "I make plenty for da all of us," she said. "Yor place is with yor husband."

Alan corrected her, "You've done enough for us, Ma. I make plenty for all of us. I've got this."

In the loving realm of his family, it didn't take Rob long to heal. Though his back wasn't at hundred percent, he got back out into the world of work. Construction companies were leery of hiring him with that injury on his medical record. Rob has two major loves in his life known as Ethel and Alan. But his two eccentric loves are his love for Becky and his love for building things. If no one was gonna hire him to build things. He had to do it on his own. So, he got out and hustled up business for himself. Everyone in Amory knew him from his childhood. They knew his skills surpassed him. Because of that, he had no problem getting contracts.

Some of those companies he had contacted about a job, heard about him bulldozing his way into their industry and decided he wasn't welcome. They started making trouble for him. Small subtle hints at first. Enough to scare some of the black folks who could afford to pay away from him. But he wouldn't be run off. Not from something he loved as much as this. When things went from subtle to extreme, people stopped requesting his services. Mostly because they were afraid for his life. They didn't want to be responsible for anything happening to him. But Rob couldn't sit around idle. That's not his character. He kept his hands busy, doing jobs for the poor people for no pay at all.

Then one day a prominent lawyer from another town knocked on his door with a proposition. "My name is Jonas P. Jonas. I'm from Pelahatchie. Just a short way up da road from ya. I've heard good things about you, young man. I came to offer you a job."

"You've got my attention," Rob said.

"I need a small house built for my daughter. A playhouse, but with everything a real house has. Electricity and all. If you do as good of a job as folks say you do, I have a few friends who could use you too. I'll put in a word," Jonas told him.

Rob thought about what Mr. Sanderford told him when he offered him his first job working for him.

'Never agree to a job unless you're okay with the pay'. "What kinda pay you offerin'?" he asked Mr. Jonas.

Jonas handed him a picture and information about the small house and then quoted him an offer. It was literally a small home actually big enough to live in. With everything Jonas wanted done to it, it will be livable. "Does that sound fair to ya?"

"Add another grand and I'll make that work," Rob replied. "This isn't somethin' I can do alone. I'll need help."

Jonas could appreciate that. In fact, he already knew the quote was too low. He was testing his knowledge of the field, so-to-speak. "I'll tell you what. If yor work is what people say it is, I promise you a fair pay above my original offer." That was good enough for Rob. He accepted the job, rounded up two more guys; Alan being one of them, and made ready for his first big money paying job.

It turned out well for Rob that Jonas was a man of his word. When the project was finished and far exceeded what he expected even after all the good talk he'd heard, he paid Rob double the quoted price which was actually the real fair price for such a project. From there Rob gave himself a name and pursued his passion full time. Hence, Low-Bar Construction was born.

Life was good for Rob. He has his wife, his mother, his friend, and his business. But time and again he found his friend in a puddle of thought. He knew the thought was of Mic. He wished Al could be as happy as he is right now.

#

Now in college herself, Michelle had her own bouts with reality. She had made up her mind that she would return home to her mom and Alan after she was done with high school. But when she got word that Alan had married her arch enemy, Azalea Wright, she decided home would be anywhere else but Amory. Beverly couldn't wait to tell her about it. "She wanted me to be one of her Bride's Maids. A lie! I told her to her face. I said Michelle is a good friend of mine. And you're marrying the man that should've been 'er husband. You can get somebody else girl…"

It seemed like Beverly was going to go on forever. Michelle really didn't want to hear the details of first love marrying someone else. "Lis'en Bev, I've gotta go. I'm workin' on college applications. Thanks for lettin' me know though." She went on to college as far away as possible from Amory and now wonders where she'll go from there.

She met a handsome doctor-in-the-making whom she once hoped would be able to sway her heart from Alan. But the more they were together, the more she found herself comparing the two. He didn't have Alan's captivating smile that made her happy inside. He couldn't tell funny jokes that made her laugh hysterically outside. He didn't have his handsome ambers that she loved staring into. And he never unpinned her hair to let it fall and fixed it to compliment her face. Eventually, she decided trying to love someone other than Alan was just too much work. She concentrated on her studies instead. Later on, she learned that her dad had a play in her meeting the good doctor-to-be. She was venting about it to her mom on the phone one evening. "I had no idea Dad could be so evil. I don't know why I'm so surprised though. After what he threatened to do to Al. Anybody who can't like someone as sweet as Alan is pure evil."

"Michy don't talk about yor father that way. He is still yor father. You have to respect that."

"I don't have any respect for 'im. I don't even know if I love 'im anymore."

Mrs. Peterson wanted to tell Michelle the truth. That Alan isn't married. That he can't even look at another woman. But that would only make her hate her father even more because he put this whole scheme together also to keep them apart. But she came as close as she could to telling her. "Michy, don't give up on Alan just yet. True love always finds a way to win."

"You think so Mom."

"I know so Baby."

"I'm glad I still have you."

"You'll always have me."

#

The more popular Low-Bar Construction became, the more the threats intensified. But Rob was determined no one would keep him from his dream. One day while on a site, Becky showed up with news that an order he needed right away was in. He and the guys were in the middle of something he couldn't leave at the moment. Becky offered to go pick up the order for him. He had no idea that his breaks had been tampered with before he left home that morning. "Are you sure? Cause I can go aft'r we finish with this," he said to her.

"By then the store will be closed. I don't mind. Really." She kissed him on the cheek and turned to leave. He pulled her back and gave her a real kiss. "You act like I'm not coming back Rob Barlow," she said playfully.

"You'd bett'r," he said. "I'm not above comin' ta look for ya."

An hour later, the sheriff shows up at the site. Rob's gut tells him he's bringing bad news. "Hello Rob."

"Sheriff," Rob spoke.

The sheriff was hesitant to speak. "I'm afraid I've got some bad news. Becky ran off da road on 'er way from da lumb'r store," he told Rob.

"Is she hurt bad?" Rob asked.

The Sheriff hesitated again. "She's gone, Rob. She lost control of da truck, hit a tree. Died instantly."

"No! No!" Rob said, as he began to cry. "Not my Becky. Not my Becky." He fell to his knees in unbelief. Alan and the guys had to help him up and get him home.

Sanderford was waiting for him with Ethel when they got there. They had already been given the news. They all knew it was Becky. But formalities had to be followed. Someone had to officially identify the body. Rob was in no shape at the moment. "Give us an hour or so," Ethel asked the officers.

"Yes Mam," one of them said. "We're all sorry about Becky, Mr. Sanderford. Real sorry."

Two days later, sheriff deputies showed up at Ethel's again. Sanderford, again was there. He's spent most of his time there since Becky's death. Rob isn't taking it well at all. He's been in his room since they returned from identifying her body. Funeral arrangements had to be tended to. Sanderford was all too familiar with the process due to the passing of Becky's parents and his own wife. But this had to be handled by Rob, him being her husband. Ethel and Alan had finally convinced him to get out of bed so he could make plans to lay his wife to rest. Sanderford was there to help him with the process.

"Good afternoon folks," the deputy spoke. "Sorry ta barge in on ya like this. There's been some new d'velopments in Becky's death."

"What kinda d'velopments?" Sanderford asked. "Rob isn't very talkative these days."

"It appears Becky's death wasn't an accident. Someone tampered with da breaks on da truck," he said. "Becky was killed by someone else's hands."

Rob was even more heartbroken. He knew at that moment that his beautiful Becky was killed because of him. "Rob," the other deputy said, "we're gonna have to take you in for questionin'."

"Now wait a minute, young fella," Sanderford interrupted, "yur not thinkin' Rob had anythin' ta do with this?"

"No sir, Mr. Sanderford. I don't think he had anythin' ta do with it at all," he answered. "But I was told to bring 'im in for questionin'. That's what I gotta do, Sir."

The other deputy added. "Da d'partment thought you'd wanna know da circumstances b'hind Becky's death, that oth'r hands w're involved." He wasn't as neighborly as his counterpart.

"I have no doubt that someone else had a play in this. But you'll have an easier job convincin' me that snow is green than you would that Rob's hands w're da ones involved. Everybody in this town knows he loves Becky senselessly. He'd nev'r do anythin' ta hurt 'er."

"Maybe not, Sir. But we still gotta take 'im in," the deputy concluded remorsefully.

They all went down to the station with Rob. But they never saw him once he entered the building.

They interrogated him for hours trying to get him to admit to killing Becky. When he wouldn't, they began beating him, expecting to get a confession that way. Sanderford, Ethel, and Alan were sent home after they were told Rob was being charged for the murder of his wife.

Outside the station, hearts were being shattered all over again. "Whatta we gon do?" Alan asked. "He didn't kill Becky! We can't leave 'im there."

"We have to for now," Sanderford said. "It's late. Nothin' can be done. My gut tells me that was on purpose."

Sanderford expected an arraignment the next morning and bale to be set. But there wasn't one. If there was no bale, he couldn't get Rob out. Alan wasn't having it. That morning, he took it upon himself to make his way to Pelahatchie to seek help from Mr. Jonas. Once again it was late, but early the next morning, he was at the sheriff's department ready to fight on Rob's behalf. They were all familiar with Jonas' reputation. They knew they didn't have a case against Rob unless he confessed. And they now knew that after three days of beatings, they weren't getting one.

When they released him into Jonas' custody, he was in dire need of medical care. Mr. Jonas looked sternly at the deputies and said, "Fellas, this young man looks like a lawsuit." Fearing for his life, they took him to a hospital in Jackson. When he was well enough to walk, he laid his wife to rest.

8

A LIFE FOR A LIFE

§

As Michelle held on to Alan's hand for dear life, his dear life; she was reminded of the struggle they endured just to have a chance to be together. There hasn't been a struggle since throughout their entire marriage in comparison. She remembered the heartbreaking news that brought her and her husband back together. She shared her memory with Alan assuring him that if that couldn't keep them apart, this couldn't either.

§

When Michelle got the call from her mom, she was ecstatic to hear from her again. That is until she learned it was the sad news of Rebecca's death. "Hi Mom!" she answered the phone. I'm so glad you called. I was just about ta call you actually...,"

"Michy," her mom interrupted. Michelle heard the sadness in her voice.

"What is it Mom?"

"There was an accident. Yor friend Becky was killed." Michelle was devastated.

"Rob?" she asked. "What about her husband Rob?"

"She was alone in da truck. She was da only one in da accident." She cried all night, wondering whether or not to return home for the funeral. What would she do if she ran into Al and Azalea? But Becky was her best friend. And Rob as well. She had to attend the funeral. It wouldn't be right if she didn't.

#

When she saw Rob at the funeral just before the services began, he was all bruised up. Al was by his side like she knew he would be. She stayed in the backdrop because she didn't want to see Azalea consoling the man who should have been her husband. But Azalea didn't appear to be there. When she was able to get close to Rob briefly, he told her the whole gruesome story behind his bruises and Becky's death.

Rob noticed her looking around, likely for Al when the service was over. "He left," he told her. "He said he couldn't stand to see you with 'im."

"With who?" she asked.

"Yor dad made sure he knew you had married and that's why you didn't r'turn home. Al always said you would be his wife."

Michelle was quiet for a spell. Trying to understand the untoward mind of her father. "I've nev'r stopped lovin' him," she confessed. "My dad lied. He tried to marry me off to one of his friend's sons who was studying to be a doctor. But I wasn't in love with him. I wasn't about to commit myself to someone I didn't love." She paused before asking, "Is that why he married Azalea?"

"Azalea," Rob repeated.

"Yeah. Beverly told me that he and Azalea had married about a year ago." The look on Rob's face told her it was all a lie also.

"Al never married Azalea or any other plant. Da only flow'r he's ev'r been interested in is you." Rob was glad to hear the lies were being cleared up that were put in place to keep them apart. He knew Al would be too. "Al would wanna hear what you just told me. You know where to find 'im."

"I'm so sorry for what hap'ened ta Becky and you. And Al and me. All b'cause of hatred." She gave him a long hug. "We'll get t'gether b'fore I leave."

Rob knew when she found Al, he wouldn't let her leave him again. "Mic, I've a feelin' yur not goin' anywhere."

"Mic," she repeated. "Nobody's called me that in years. I've missed that."

"Me too."

She found Alan sitting under the trestle, just where she figured he'd be. He sat looking out over the pasture with his back to her. He didn't hear her walk up. But he recognized her perfume from the early years. "Did you bring yor fancy doctor husband ta show 'im how trussell rats live?"

"No," she replied. "My husband's already h're." Her voice was as sweet as his last memory of it. Her high pitch twang never sounded so good. He immediately stood and turned to greet her. "How'd you know it was me?"

"You still wear da same perfume." She smiled. *'The good doctor doesn't do that either',* she thought, staring into his handsome ambers. "You didn't get married to some doctor student?" he asked.

"No." she answered.

"Yor father said…"

She interrupted. "Yeah, Rob told me. Beverly told me you had married off too. That's why I didn't come home. I didn't wanna see you with someone else."

"So, we w're both lied to," he concluded.

"To keep us apart," Michelle added. "I can't believe my dad."

Alan got himself a good long look at Michelle. Then he pulled her close to him and hugged her like there was no tomorrow. When he finally let her go, he removed the pin from her hair to let it fall to her shoulders. Then he fixed it to the shape of her face. "Yur still da prettiest girl in school ta me."

"Except school is ov'r," she added. They smiled.

"Yes it is," Alan said. "And now no one can keep us apart. Marry me, Mic."

"What, I don't get no fancy romantic dinn'r?" she teased.

"Da last time I tried that, you disappeared inta thin air. I'm not takin' that chance again," he said.

"When my dad said he was gonna send me away, my mom told me that if you truly loved me, you would wait for me."

He laughed. "Rob said that you would come home as soon as you w're able. And when you did, you wouldn't stop until you found me."

"I've waited all my life to marry you, Amber Eyes," Michelle said. "Da soon'r, da bett'r."

\#

As sad as Alan and Mic were over Becky's death, this was the happiest day of their lives. Until that is, Michelle told her parents she was going to marry Alan like she should've done years ago. Alan wouldn't let her face her parents alone or leave his sight again for that matter. He stood by her side throughout the whole ordeal. Her mother was happy for her. She knew Alan was waiting for her. Now her daughter could be happy.

Things got ugly with Mr. Peterson though. He was furious and he directed all of his anger towards Alan. "You just couldn't let 'er be, could you? What kinda life is she gonna have with you? You came from nowhere and nowhere is where you'll end up!" he screamed at Alan.

"Dad, stop it!" Michelle screamed in return.

"Jeffrey!" Mrs. Peterson said. "Yur being unreasonable."

"You keep outta this, Val! This is between me and da trussell rat!"

There were so many things Alan wanted to say to Mr. Peterson. But he didn't want to hurt Michelle any more than she was already hurting. Her own father was doing an excellent job of that all by himself.

Michelle realized that Alan would just stand and take her father's abuse for her sake. She wasn't going to let that continue so she took hold of his hand and said, "Come on Al. Let's go."

She gave her mother a hug and turned to walk away. "Michy if you walk out that door with this riffraff, yor mother and I will nev'r speak to you again." Michelle knew her mother didn't share her dad's feelings. She could see it in her eyes. They were filled with just as much pain as her own.

"Then I guess this is good-bye, Daddy," she said.

#

Michelle tried to pretend all was well when they made it to Ma Ethel's house. Alan told them what happened because Michelle didn't want to talk about it. Ethel fixed her some chamomile tea and got her settled in Alan's bedroom. The next morning, they all went down to the Justice of Peace Office to marry off Alan and Michelle. It was a small gathering of their family and only their closest friends. Of course, the Marshalls were in attendance. They weren't about to miss their only son's marriage.

Sanderford was happy to see something pleasant come out of Becky's death. He even made mention of it to Alan and Michelle. "Becky told me she asked you to be her maid of honor. She didn't have one b'cause you couldn't be there. I can feel 'er smilin' right now at you two. I'm so happy for ya. I know she is too." Before he left for the evening, he made mention to Ethel that he was tired and had some rest to catch up on. Ethel told him she understood and that she would call him tomorrow before bringing lunch over. "Do that!" he said. "Good night y'all." He gave all of them extra-long hugs before leaving.

That night as he danced with his beautiful forbidden wife, Alan swore secretly that Michelle would never regret defying her father to marry him. He promised she would never miss the life she was accustomed to growing up. And that she would always be the only woman he would ever love. But there was one thing he promised her openly, "One day, I'm gonna give you a weddin' as grand as Becky's was. I promise you." That was all well and good to Michelle for the future, but she was more than content with the present, snuggled in her husband's arms.

"Al, what could be dreamier than this?" she asked raising her head from his chest.

#

Just as she promised, Ethel tried to connect with Sanderford to bring his lunch over, but he didn't answer his phone. Rob was lying on the sofa trying to rest. Ethel hated to bother him. But that was her third call. "Robert," she said. "Something's wrong. Whit's not answerin' da phone."

"Maybe he's sleepin' in," Rob told her.

"I don't know. I'm gonna go check on 'im," she said.

"Check on who?" Alan asked when he and Michelle entered the room.

"Ma's been callin' Sanderford all mornin' but not getting' an answer," Rob explained.

Alan didn't like the sound of that. "And why are we still h're?" he asked.

They all accompanied Ethel to his house to check on him. They found him lounged in his favorite chair. He was clutching a photo to his chest of the four of them from the early years, resting in eternal sleep. He still had the same clothes on from last night. He couldn't get past the heartache of losing his precious granddaughter. With her gone, there was no reason for him to hang around. He quietly drifted away in his sleep. Ethel hadn't understood last night. But she fully understands now. Once again in less than a week, the graveyard beckoned for a visit.

#

Calls had been coming in from ear to ear from people needing things built, from houses to multi-level buildings to large complexes. When Rob and Alan got back to work they had more work than they could handle. Low-Bar Construction took off like a whirlwind, accelerating in speed with each passing day. Rob put all he had left into his company. He built an empire of something he loved dearly on the excruciating pain of losing someone he loved even more. He needed every bit of work that came his way to get over losing Becky. Still, it wasn't enough.

Alan and Mic looked into buying a home on the other side of town, but Rob made mention that he was thinking about relocating. The pain was unbearable for him. And Ethel as well. It was as if the pain of losing Becky wasn't enough. But the pain of losing the only father figure he had ever had in his life, had to be included in the real-feel deal. He pondered on the thought for nearly a month, hoping they could actually get over it.

Alan and Mic changed their minds about buying a house and decided to rent instead. They rented the big house not very far from her parents until decisions about moving were finalized. Alan had made up his mind that wherever Rob goes, he's going too. They've been through too much together. Rob needed him more now than ever before.

The thought weighed so heavily on Rob one day at work until he just had to talk to Ethel about it. He wanted to know what she wanted to do. He went home on his lunch break to find her missing in action. She had long since relieved herself of her community services so there was no reason for her not to be home. He continued on to the only other place she could be. He found her cleaning the place as if she expected him to come home to it. She started talking as soon as he walked in. "Look at all this dust. It's amazing how it collects everywhere. It gets all ov'r everythin'. There ain't no windows or doors open. Where's it all comin' from?" she babbled on.

"Ma, you don't have to clean this up. Al and I can get it," Rob told her.

"Ain't no need for a man ta do a woman's work when a woman's plenty capable of doin' it 'erself," she defended without stopping.

"Ma," he grabbed her by the shoulders, "this can wait. Let's go home." By the time they made it home, Ethel was crying hysterically. He made her a cup of tea and put her to bed. Then he called Alan to tell him he wouldn't be coming back to work today and asked if he and Mic could come over afterwards.

That evening when Al and Mic arrived, Rob was hanging up from a last phone call with a realtor. "What's going on Rob? Where's Ma Ethel?" they asked when they didn't see her anywhere.

"In 'er bedroom restin'," Rob answered.

"I'll go sit with 'er while you two talk," Mic suggested.

"I've made up my mind," Rob started. "I'm sellin' everythin' and movin' away from h're."

"What happened?" Alan asked.

"When I came home for lunch, she wasn't h're. She was ov'r ta Sanderford's cleanin' like he was still there. By da time we got back to da house, she was in full blown hysterics."

"Awe, man," Alan replied.

"There's too much pain h're, Al. We've gotta go."

"Well, you needn't think yur gonna leave Mic and me h're. We're right b'hind ya."

"Just what I wanted to hear. I wouldn't feel comfortable leavin' you two h're alone. Not when da whole town may be against ya."

"Not da whole town," he said referring to the Marshalls.

Rob immediately put both houses up for sale. Rob has learned to trust his gut instincts. When they happened upon a small township just outside of Natchez, something felt right about it. So, he bought Ethel a nice flat in Saint Catherine; the small, picturesque township one hundred and eighty miles away from Amory. That's where he stayed until his own home would be completed, The Greystone. It would be a beautifully designed original, crafted from his own head and settling an entire block all on its own. It would represent everything he's building for himself.

Alan and Michelle found the perfect home about twenty minutes away from where Rob was building. A magnificent southern heritage home beautifully constructed and just two nails shy of being a mansion. Mic fell in love with it at first sight. "This place is beautiful," she spoke softly; emotionally responding to its ambience. She was already picturing them happily evolved in it evident of the smile that brushed across her face. It far exceeded in style and beauty the first home they looked at when they arrived in the new city. Michelle liked that one also. Rob didn't think it was worth what the owners were asking for it, but they wouldn't budge on the price. Now, she was glad the owners were being stubborn.

Alan noticed Mic's smile and imagined her picturing their future together in it. "This house is much more suitable for you," Alan told her. "I can't wait to have lots of babies ta fill it up with."

Michelle, mimicking Alan's associated humor said, "Ok. But can we buy da place first and enjoy da process of fillin it with babies?"

"Oh yeah," Al agreed smiling, "we definitely can do that."

#

One year later Ethel was settled in her new home. Rob's massive mansion was near completion. And Al and Mic had begun talks about having children. All is right in the universe, Alan thought. But he was concentrating so much on trying to help Rob through his bereavement, he didn't noticed Michelle having mild medical symptoms. Michelle didn't mention them to him because she didn't want to worry him especially since he was so concerned about Rob. The stress of missing her mom and hating her dad for causing her to miss her, had put a significant strain on her heart.

She began experiencing occasional chest pains and shortness of breath. It would have gone completely unnoticed if Alan hadn't come home from work one evening during one of her attacks. This one was worse than any of the others. He walked into the kitchen to find her slumped over the counter trying desperately to catch her breath. His first thought was that she was choking on something. When he asked her, she shook her head vigorously. Not knowing how long she had been this way; he didn't bother to call an ambulance. He rushed her to the emergency room himself. By the time they arrived, she was so exhausted from trying to breathe, she had passed out. They immediately rushed her away. "What's her name?" the nurse asked as they began to roll her away.

"Michelle," Alan answered. "Michelle Ferguson."

"Who are you?"

"Her husband," he replied.

"Mr. Ferguson, they need you at da desk. We'll take good care of her," the nurse said.

He called Rob before starting the paperwork to let him know. He could barely concentrate, but he didn't know many of the answers about her family's medical history anyway. So, he handed the nearly blank paperwork back to the clerk and he returned to the waiting area where Rob and Ethel were waiting. "What hap'ened?" Rob asked.

"I don't know. She was havin' trouble breathin' when I got home." Al said frantically. "She passed out just b'fore we got h're."

"Did she choke on somethin'?" Ethel asked.

"I asked her. She shook 'er head, no."

"Try not to worry, Sweetheart," Ethel told him. "She'll be alright."

They all sat quietly waiting for what seemed like hours for someone to come out and tell them what's happening with her. Alan paced the floor walking from his chair to the window and back to the chair again. He turned quickly when he heard his name called. "Mr. Ferguson?"

"Right h're. How is she? Is she alright?" he asked anxiously.

"She's breathing comfortably now," the doctor said. "Does yor wife have a history of heart disease in da family?

"I don't know. I don't know about 'er family history."

"Has she been complainin' of chest pains or shortness of breath?"

"No. Nothin' like that." Alan spoke in frustration. "Why? What's wrong with 'er?"

"Mrs. Ferguson has developed a heart condition called coronary heart disease," the doctor said.

"What? How?" Alan asked.

"Stress is a major factor among a few other things. Has she been under any stress lately? Are the two of you havin' any problems?"

Alan was immediately taken back to her father. And his demeanor changed from concern to anger. "We haven't been havin' problems, but she probably has been stressed out. She nev'r mentioned it to me though."

"How so?" the doctor asked.

"We've only been married just ov'r a year. Her dad didn't approve. He banned her from her home and her mom. She hasn't seen or spoken to 'er mom since we w're married."

"I see. What's she like around da house? Is she sleepin'?"

"Now that you mention it, no. She keeps herself busy all day with da house and at bedtime she watches late night shows. I watch with 'er until I fall asleep."

"That sounds about right," the doctor said.

"Can you fix her?" Alan asked the doctor.

"We're certainly gonna try," he said. "I'm gonna prescribe her a couple of medications. We'll start there. Her heart's in a pretty weakened state. So be patient. In da meantime, you can go in to see 'er."

"All of us?" he asked.

"She'll be glad to see all of ya."

After giving her the longest hug ever in the history of their relationship, Alan cautiously scolded her. "Why didn't you tell me you w're hurtin'? And that you w're missin' yor mom so much."

"I didn't want you to think that I wasn't happy with you. I didn't want you to think that you w'ren't enough," Mic explained.

"I wouldn't have thought that," he replied. "I know you love yor mom. I care about what's best for you, Mic and yor happiness. You'll always come first with me. Always."

"I know that." Mic said. "Da problem is though, is that you'll always come first with me too. Besides, you couldn't have done anythin'. Dad won't let 'er have anythin' ta do with me. At least, I hope that's what it is. I hope she hasn't sided with him now."

"Why would think that?" Alan asked her.

"I tried to call her just b'fore we moved to tell 'er we were leaving. The phone kept disconnecting. I've sent her lett'rs. But she doesn't answer them. What else could it be?"

"I'm sure that was yor Dad. I saw the look on yor mom's face. She wouldn't turn on you." Then he thought about her dilemma. Don't worry Mic. We'll figure out somethin'," Alan said, "ta reconnect you and yor mom."

"Mic, I'm sorry too if I've let my issues interfere with Al carin' for you," Rob told her. "That will nev'r hap'en again. His first priority is to you. I'm gonna see ta that from now on."

"I'll see ta that too, Baby," Ethel added. "We're not gonna lose you too."

They admitted Michelle to keep watch on her heart for a while. A while turned into two weeks and two weeks into four. Each time her heart seemed to be getting stronger, the chest pains and shortness of breath would return. Alan tried to reach out to the Petersons to let them know what was going on with Michelle, but by now their number had been changed to an unlisted private number. He promised her that as soon as she was home he would go back to Amory to talk to her mom. Michelle refused to allow him to do that for fear of what her father might do to him. She never told Alan about the threat her dad made towards him when she was sent away.

Michelle didn't know that Mrs. Peterson had tried diligently to connect with her also. When she found out they had moved into the big house, she visited them when she could get away from her husband. She didn't want him to know where they were living. She was sure he would cause trouble for them. But each time she visited the big house, no one was home.

Getting away was no longer a problem for a while after Mrs. Peterson left her husband temporarily. She came home one day from the big house miserable and hurting for her daughter. Mr. Peterson had been looking for her. He met her at the door. "Where have you been? I've been lookin' all ov'r for you."

"You mean like I've been lookin' for my daughter," she answered.

"Is that where you've been running off to all this time?" he snapped. "I won't have any more of that. I forbid it! Michelle made her choice. Now da both of you will have to live with it."

The hurt and anger had magnified so much inside her that she couldn't stand the sight of him any longer. "My daughter wasn't given a choice. Her own father pushed her away. She couldn't enjoy her friends in high school b'cause she knew you wouldn't approve of 'em. That's why she nev'r brought them to da house. She wasn't ashamed of them. She was ashamed of you! She was da happiest I've ev'r seen her when she was with her new friends."

"Whatta you mean by that? You saw her with those low lifes. And you didn't tell me."

"That's right, Jeffrey. One of her parents needed to look out for 'er happiness. You certainly haven't done a very good job of that. I can't stand da sight of you anymore. I'm leavin'."

"And just where do you think yur gonna go?" he asked her.

"Maybe I'll bed-up und'r da railroad trestle. Anywhere is bett'r than being h're with you."

She packed only a few things right then. She made her way to a friend's house and stayed there hoping Michelle would try to reach her. But she didn't. After a while, Mr. Peterson fell sick and couldn't do for himself, so she returned home six months later to take care of him. After he was better, she decided she was too old to be single and stayed with him for comfort's sake.

When Low-Bar Construction took off in the whirlwind, business was all over the place. Rob and Al traveled wherever business took them. When Alan left, Mic went with him. So, Mrs. Peterson was never able to connect with her daughter while they lived in the big house. Now that they've moved, she has no idea where they've gone. But that didn't stop her from trying. She tried to send letters to Michelle at the address of the big house asking her to forgive her father. She hoped they would be forwarded to wherever she is now. Mr. Peterson, however, clearly unaffected by the ill-health he had not long ago recovered from; confiscated the letters before the postman could get them. He was hell-bent on keeping Michelle away from her mother and out of her life. It was his punishment to her. It was as though, if Michelle wouldn't be a part of his life, she wasn't going to be a part of her mother's life either. He was completely blind to the fact that he wasn't just hurting his daughter. He was also hurting the woman he proclaimed to love and cherish 'til death do them part.

#

After her month-long stay in the hospital, Michelle was eventually allowed to go home under the conditions of provided home health care. Ethel wasn't about to have her staying home all alone all day in between nurse's visits while Alan was working. "You have two choices, Baby," Ethel said. "You can come home with me until yur strong enough to care for yorself or I can come stay with you."

"Those aren't bad choices," Alan agreed. "I'd feel bett'r knowin' Ma Ethel's with you."

"That makes three of us," Rob said.

"That sounds like a good idea Mrs. Ferguson," the doctor said. "You'll be very limited for a while as to what you'll be able to do. Even tasks as simple as laundry or cooking would be off limits for now. A couple of extra hands would do you good."

Michelle looked at them all while they explained why she should have the only mother-figure in her life around her right now when she needs her as badly as she does. She finally said, "Y'all don't have to sell me on Ma Ethel. I couldn't get through this without 'er. I'm glad I didn't have to ask her. I can stay with you while Al is workin' and go home with him when he gets in from work."

Alan was up before daybreak sometimes to get to work. He felt like that would be too much for her each day. "No," he said, "We'll stay with Ma for a while."

At the recommendation of her doctor, they put off their dream of having a family until they were sure her heart could handle it.

§

Michelle gently squeezed his hand and said to him, "Those were da toughest times we've ev'r had to face. Until now. But we got through them. Just like we're gonna get through this." She wasn't sure if he could hear her. And if he could, she hoped her reminiscing didn't upset him. It's amazing the comfort a simple gesture can bring. Like the one she experienced when he gently squeezed her hand in return. Likely, agreeing with her.

9

Empty For A Season

Alan remembered all too well the trying times he and Mic experienced the first twelve years of their marriage. He followed along in his mind as Mic continued walking backwards in time down a road they once dreaded. A road that unexpectantly took a turn for the better. She kissed his hand and continued in tears. Much like the tears at the beginning of their bumpy road. But quite different from those in the end.

"Do you r'member how afraid you w're for me when you found out you w're gonna be a daddy?" she started. She smiled as if he could see her. "There was nothin' you could've said ta me to make me give up yor baby. Seeing the joy that he's brought to you now, to both of us, aren't you glad I'm so stubborn? I'll nev'r forget how

Ma Ethel helped me realize how I was hurtin' myself and you. How I played a part in keepin' us from havin' a family. I'll nev'r forget da day we found out that was about to b'come a reality."

§

Now, with the disappointment of not being able to start a family right away, Michelle had an even heavier weight on her heart. She didn't think she could hate her father any more than she did already, but she has since learned differently. Once again, she secretly cried when Alan wasn't around saddened that she might never be able to give him a family.

Ethel heard her one autumn day out on the back porch sobbing uncontrollably. She walked up behind her, put her hand on her back gently caressing it. "It's okay ta miss yor mom, Baby," Ethel said. "But you can't let it consume you this way."

Michelle turned to hug Ethel. She held her long and tight. When she finally let go, she wiped her eyes and shared a confession with her. "I'm not cryin' b'cause I miss my mom. I'm cryin' b'cause I hate my dad. He wanted to hurt Alan cause he hates him. He wanted to hurt me b'cause I love 'im. He's succeeded in all his hatred ta do exactly what he set out to do. And I hate 'im for it. I didn't even think it was possible to hate yor own parent."

"What has he done, Mic?"

"He broke my heart by takin' my mom away from me. Now it can't be fixed. As long as my heart is broken, I'll nev'r be able to give Alan a family of his own," Mic explained. "Family is important to 'im. More important than anythin' else."

Ethel sat her down on the porch swing where she joined her. With one arm around her shoulder, she pointed to the bare trees in the distance. "Look out there," she said. "Tell me what you see?"

"Emptiness," Michelle answered. "Empty trees, empty flowerbeds. Everything's empty ... just like me."

"Empty for a season," Ethel told her. "They're only empty for a season. Just like you. Forgiveness is da beginnin' of healin'. Allow yorself to forgive yor father and yor season will begin to change."

"I don't know if I can," Mic confessed.

"You don't have a choice. Yor heart is demanding it of you. You've let 'im take yor joy and yor health. Are you gonna let 'im take yor life too?" Mic gave a strange look at Ethel. Like she had just turned a corner and entered into a different zone full of light and clarity. A realm of newfound understanding.

"Thank you, Ma," she said. "No. I won't let 'im take my life. I won't leave Al alone. He'd rather have the real deal," she said referring to the locket she gave him when they were teenagers, which, he still wears daily. Then she smiled at Ethel. "Will you help me fix dinn'r for my husband?"

"I wouldn't enjoy anything more," Ethel said.

Later that evening at dinner, Alan, and Rob both saw a difference in Michelle that they couldn't quite put their finger on. She seemed relieved or something related to that. He was too curious to wait until they were in private. "Mic, you look wonderful Sweetheart. Are you feelin' bett'r?" he asked her.

"Yes," she answered.

"Did somethin' hap'en taday?" he asked again.

"Yes," she answered again. Alan put his fork down and sat back in his chair. Rob sat back in his as well.

He wanted to know what was going on with her also. Michelle looked up from her plate. "I cooked dinn'r taday."

"I thought this tasted familiar." he said, looking at Ethel. Ethel grinned and nodded. "That's great, Baby but..."

"Da trees are empty," she interrupted. "I'm ready to go home."

Alan was completely confused. Michelle was making no sense at all. She could see that in his expression, so she made things clearer for him. "Ma Ethel made me realize that my dad is only partially responsible for what's hap'ning ta me. I'm responsible for da oth'r part. I love you Al. I fell in love with you da very first day I looked into yor handsome ambers. I've never loved anyone else since. I won't let my dad taint my love for you any long'r. I may nev'r be able to stop missin' my mom. But I'm gonna try my best to forgive my dad so that my season of emptiness can change." She paused, taking another bite of food. "Can we go home?"

"Yeah," he said, "t'night even."

#

Eventually, Alan and Mic came to terms with the truth that they would never have children of their own. They decided they would adopt as soon as Mic's heart was strong enough. They both were so afraid for her life that they could never come to a definitive conclusion that it is already. As fate would have it, they had waited long enough for their family.

After another one of her chest pain attacks, Mic was rushed to the hospital again. The symptoms began right after breakfast. When she placed her hand to her chest, Alan immediately rushed her to the hospital. "Al, it's not that serious. Really," she told him on the way.

"I'm not takin' any chances, Mic." He drove like a maniac.

"Al, slow down. Please." She pleaded with her husband.

He was so afraid for her. But he didn't want to put more pressure on her heart. So, he slowed to a more acceptable speed. "I'm sorry. I don't mean to scare you. I just wanna make sure yur alright."

Once the doctor finished his examination and all the test were back, they learned that she was only experiencing a bad case of heartburn associated with carrying her first baby. When Dr. Westland told them about the baby, Alan became fearful for his wife all over again. "Doc. Can she carry a pregnancy? How will this affect her heart?"

Dr. Westland fully understood his concerns. He had his own as well. He spoke to both of them. Mr. Ferguson, Mrs. Ferguson. Of corse I can't make this decision for you. Yor heart is still very weak. It's made some progress. Whether or not that progress is enough to sustain childbirth," he paused. "I just don't know. My professional suggestion would be not to chance it. But like I said, this has to be yor decision."

Michelle felt stronger than she had felt in a very long time. She was overjoyed about the baby. Before he could say what she knew he was thinking, she made it clear to him, "I'm keepin' our baby."

"But Mic..." he began to plead.

"My season has changed Al," she said. "It's taken twelve years. If I have to lay in this hospital bed for da duration of this pregnancy connected to machines every single hour, I'm havin' our baby."

Alan knew better than to try to reason with her. They both wanted this baby. But he wanted his wife too to help raise it. His best option was to support her and make sure she was as comfortable and stress free as possible.

Once again, Ethel came to the rescue, moving in with them so that she could be comfortable in her own home until she was ready to deliver. Mrs. Marshall wouldn't leave them hanging in the wind either. She joined Ethel in taking care of Michelle. Alan took a vacation from going on the road to work and stayed close to Mic. It certainly wasn't a carefree pregnancy. Even though she was diligent in being careful, for her heart's sake, there were many bed-ridden days. Some, even at the hospital. But Michelle was determined to give Alan the family he wants.

Alan could see a big difference in Michelle than that of previous years. A much happier Mic, even with the trouble that came with her pregnancy. He felt compelled to share that with her. She was resting on the porch, caressing her belly, and smiling. He sat down beside her and put his hand atop hers. "You look amazing Mic. So happy and stress free. You don't know how long I've wanted to see you happy again."

"What about you, Al? Are you happy too?"

"More than I could ev'r express."

Their happiness turned to an overwhelming joy even with the trouble that accompanied the pregnancy, and it was all deemed worth it when she placed Alan Junior in his father's arms for the first time. It started a bond that would only grow stronger and reseal itself over and over again through the years.

Alan was in tears, holding his namesake that for years he thought he'd never have. "Hi Little Guy," he said just before a gentle kiss on his little forehead. "Welcome home."

Michelle smiled and corrected, "We're not home yet, Al. We're still at da hospital."

Alan re-corrected Mic, "Any time he's in my arms, he's home no matt'r where we are."

"That's what I'm talkin' about," Michelle said smiling.

§

The memory of his son sent him into a movement frenzy. He hadn't heard AJ's voice since he had been in the hospital. If he could just hear his sweet voice, maybe he would develop the strength to come out of the darkness and back into the light. His movement was so frantic, Michelle called for the nurse.

His heartbeat had increased slightly. And he refused to let go of Michelle's hand when he was asked to do so. One of the nurses tried to communicate with him. "Mr. Ferguson can you hear me?" He squeezed Michelle's hand in response.

"He squeezed my hand," Michelle told her.

"Can you let go of your wife's hand?" she asked. He did. But then, immediately grabbed hold again. When Dr. Pelonoski came in an hour later, he concluded Alan should be in the room with his wife.

Eventually his grip on her hand weakened. She imagined he must be sleeping. The nurse informed her that it was probably a good time for her to get some rest also. She hated to leave him but, she was comforted by the fact that he would soon be sharing her room with her.

Once again Michelle was in tears. But this time a happy kaleidoscope of tears. She called Chasidy at the hotel to share the good news. She began talking as soon as Chasidy answered. "Chasidy!" She said excitedly. "Yur not gonna b'lieve this! No. Wait. Yes you will. You w're right!" Michelle was carrying on so that she was doing more rambling than talking.

"Mic. Calm down and talk slowly in full sentences," Chasidy ordered.

"Ok." Michelle took a deep breath. "Are you near Rob and AJ?"

"Yes I am. Should I put you on speaker?"

"Yes," she said definitely.

"Ok. Talk to us girl."

"You w're right about Al. He did need me with him. I stayed with 'im all day talkin' to 'im, holdin' his hand, caressin his face. About three hours ago he started respondin'. First with a hand squeeze like with you and Rob. And about an hour after that his eyelids began to move. After that, they called the doctor to check on 'im." She stopped, likely to catch her breath for she had begun to cry again. Then she continued. "He's not awake yet, but they're movin' him to my room so we can be togeth'r. Chasidy, da doctor said he could be comin' out of da coma. I just had to call and thank you."

AJ started crying also. "Mom, does that mean I can see 'im now?"

"Yes, Baby. That's exactly what it means," she told him. Mr. Peterson listened to her conversation with them, taking mental notes.

"Uncle Rob. Can you take me t'morrow?"

Rob was concerned about that. He remembered the affect the first glance of Al had on them. "Are you sure that's a good idea. R'member yor r'action when you first saw 'im?" he asked Mic.

"My son is much strong'r than I am. And besides, if Al will wade through hell and high waters ta bring me home; he'll pry open da Pearlie Gates 'imself to get back to his son. Bring 'im to see his dad," she demanded.

"Okay," Rob surrendered. They had only just the day before agreed on Alan's strong will towards his family. She could be on to something. "I think we'll all come. See ya t'morrow."

By now, her body was wreaking with pain from having no medications and she had no choice but to take something. Her father had an opinion about that. "You shouldn't go without yor medicines for so long. That can't be good for ya. Look at how much pain yur in."

'Now you're concerned about my pain,' Michelle thought. But she said, "I can't take of my husband with all those meds in me. But I'll have da nurse bring me somethin' now."

"That's what the staff is for. You should be thinking about yur own health." Her father was being his usual insensitive self. Michelle was too happy to allow him to ruin that for her. See ignored his comment.

But her mother couldn't let it pass. "Do you ever get tired of being a jack? Let my daughter be happy for once."

"She's our daughter."

"Then act like it!" Michelle smiled at her mom.

The medicine put her straight to sleep. When she awakened the next morning, she saw her husband lying in a bed next to hers. She slept so hard; she never heard them bring him in. A glorious sight for her weary eyes. She slowly climbed out of bed to render him a soft kiss on the forehead. His senses were immediately awakened. "I have a surprise for you," she said. "Rob is bringin AJ today to visit with you." She kissed him once more. "I won't tire you out this mornin'. You keep yor strength for yor son."

When AJ arrived later that day, he ran straight past his mom to his dad. Giving him the biggest hug, he possibly could, he immediately began talking to Alan. "Dad, I've missed you so much. I thought I wasn't gonna see you again. Nobody would tell me anything about you. Until Uncle Rob and Aunt Chasidy got here. I was so scared. Please wake up. And come back to me and mom."

Hearing AJ's voice even in its frantic state reminded him once again of the joy he and Michelle felt after his birth. And how she yearned even more for her mom to be a part of her life. He was even more pleased when he heard Mrs. Peterson's voice in the room. He was reminded of when she saw AJ's picture for the first time just earlier this year. He wishes now that he had followed his first mind and reached out to her so that AJ could've enjoyed his young life with his grandmother.

§

He knew Michelle wanted to share the news of AJ's birth with her mom, so he hired a private investigator to find out how to reach her. He had promised her he wouldn't go back to Amory. But never promised he wouldn't try to connect with her mother. It was a beautiful thought. But once the information was in his possession, the thought became frightening. The last thing he wanted to do was hurt his wife who had already been hurt enough for an entire lifetime. He decided then wasn't the right time. The bigger problem was that he didn't know when the right time would be. He held onto that information for another twelve years. He finally decided to use it for AJ's twelfth birthday when he invited them to his birthday celebration. Three days before the event, he got cold shoulders again.

When AJ's beloved Grandma Ethel passed only a few shorts months ago, it was difficult getting over her death. They started visiting the Marshalls on a more regular basis, hoping they could fill the gap left in his heart. It worked well enough when he was with them. He enjoyed trips to the KCS Railroad museum that Papa Stan would take him to. Papa Stan has always been fascinated with trains. But AJ enjoyed even more than that the river boat rides along the Mississippi River. His grandpa would share a different story with him each time of his early years as a riverboat captain.

But living so far away made them parttime Grands also. AJ was used to spending countless hours with Ma Ethel. Alan thought if he met his other grandparents, between the two sets; it would become easier for him. But he began however, to second guess himself. He needed his friends to help sort things out. He took a walk one evening and found himself at Barlow's front porch. Barlow and Chasidy were relaxing in the rockers when he walked up. Alan immediately commented. "It's a nice eve'nin' for that," he said. Rob could see immediately that he came with a mission. "Rob, I need to talk to you?"

"I'll go get y'all some tea," Chasidy said, also noticing a seriousness about him.

"Bring three glasses," Alan said. "I'd like to hear yor thoughts too."

"I'll be right back," she said.

Barlow hadn't seen Alan this upset since the kidnapping. Aside from Ethel's death, that is. He could hardly wait for Chasidy to get back with the tea.

Alan relieved her of the tray when she returned. "What is it? You look like yur on da run from somebody," Barlow told him.

"I might be, in three days," he replied. "From Mic." He sat down at the table with his glass of tea. "I did somethin' I thought was a good idea at first. But now I'm not so sure. I don't wanna hurt Mic."

"What did you do?" Barlow asked out of concern.

"Let me explain," Alan said. "AJ is having such a hard time with Ma Ethel's death; I thought maybe getting to know his oth'r grandparents would help 'im get through it bett'r."

Barlow set his glass down on the table. "You didn't," he said. Then he dropped his head in thought. Chasidy listened attentively.

"I did," Al replied. "I thought it would be good for 'im and well, Mic too. It's been twenty-four years since she's seen her parents. I know she misses them."

"Wait," Chasidy finally spoke. "Mic's parents are still alive?"

"Alive and kickin'," Alan told her.

"But she neva talks about 'em," Chasidy continued.

"That's why I wanted you to hear this too. I'd like yor opinion when I'm done. She sat back positioning herself for the full story. "I'm takin' AJ and a few of his friends to a rodeo on the Natchez Trace for his birthday. I thought it would be an added surprise for 'im to meet his grandparents for da first time. But I'm really hoping they can make amends with Mic too. I wanted to do this a long time ago. But I didn't have da guts."

"Sounds like they're slippin' away from ya now," Rob told him.

"They are. I've nev'r done anythin' like this b'fore without talkin' ta Mic first. But that's what makes it a surprise, right?" He chuckled and then reiterated, "But I don't wanna hurt her. I'd rath'r pull my own arm right outta da socket." Chasidy giggled at that. But Rob remembered how hurt Al and Mic were when they were separated. He remembered the terrible things Mr. Peterson said to Alan and the lies he had practically the whole town telling just to keep them apart. He didn't know much else about him. But that alone was plenty. If it were up to him he would buy AJ a set of grandparents before he allowed Mr. Peterson into his life.

Everyone was quiet for a moment. Chasidy broke the silence. "Why are they at odds with each otha'?" she asked Alan.

Alan spoke solemnly. "I wasn't her father's first choice of marriage for his only daught'r. Havin' been branded a trussell rat from takin' up lodging und'r a railroad track, I wasn't good enough for her. He vowed nev'r to speak to her again if she married me."

"That's a horrible thing for a parent ta do," Chasidy said. She completely omitted the part about him living under a railroad track. "When you spoke with 'im, did he sound like he had changed his mind about you and Mic?"

"I only talked with her dad for a short while. I couldn't tell. And I really don't care what he thinks of me. But Mic is his daught'r," he paused. "Anyway, he was very excited about meetin AJ. I remember her mother didn't seem to have any issues with us being together. She was afraid that had changed over da years though. Like maybe her dad had turned her against 'er."

"If I'm being to forward," Chasidy asked, "Why were you living under a railroad trussell? Did you and Rob have a fallan' out?"

They both grinned at that. "That's a different story. But long story short, I was homeless b'fore I met Rob and my temporary parents." Hearing that broke Chasidy's heart. Al stared a pleading glance between his friends. Rob, until now, had sat quietly listening to him and Chasidy. "Rob, whatta you thinkin'?"

"I was just about ta ask you that?" Barlow replied.

"Chasidy?" Al asked for her opinion.

"What's botherin' you more; that you invited them or that you didn't talk to Mic about it first?" she asked him.

Alan hadn't thought about that. "I don't know," he answered. "I think the latter."

"Does AJ know this story?" Chasidy asked. And then reminded him, "Have you noticed how crazy he is about his parents?"

He looked at Barlow for his input. "I think you know what you need to do," he said. "But b'fore you do, you need ta ask ya'self if want his kind of attitude influencing yor son if they b'come close."

Alan always tries to view things from the positive side. "Maybe he's changed aft'r all these years." Then he pulled out his phone, "Hey Bae, I'm ov'r to Rob's. Can you and AJ come ov'r?"

They were all staring at her with pitiful eyes as she walked up. She hadn't seen this much sadness on the porch since they lost Ethel. She assumed her husband was the culprit. "Al, what'd you do?"

Alan gave a non-admitting grin at that and invited her to the table with him. He had her glass of tea waiting for her. Reaching it to her, he said, "H're. Have some tea."

She knew it had to be serious. They don't have tea for just any old conversation. She received the glass and sat it down in front of her. "What's this about Al?"

The minute Alan revealed that he had contacted her parents, she withdrew into total silence.

AJ was perched on the step but got up and went over to his mom when heard what his dad said. "Mom, you have parents?"

Michelle began to cry. "Yes, baby. I have parents. And you have grandparents."

"I have grandparents. That's cool!" But AJ didn't understand his mother's tears. "Mom, why are you cryin'?"

She wiped her face with her hand and regained her composure. "Well, yor dad opened this can of worms. I'm gonna let him sort 'em out for ya," she said.

Alan explained how he wasn't his grandparents' first choice to be their daughter's husband. Again, AJ didn't understand that. As far as he is concerned, he has the best dad in the world. When Alan finished telling the story, he asked AJ if he wanted to meet his grandparents. AJ told him, "No." Then he said to his mother in his adorable mannerism, "Don't cry Mom. Yur happy with me and Dad, right?" Michelle nodded her head vigorously, pulling him to her for a hug.

Once again, Alan pulled out his phone. This time to call Mr. Peterson. "Alan, I'm glad you called. Val and I are so excited about seein' our grandson this weekend."

"That's why I'm callin', Mr. Peterson. There's been a change in plans. Mic can't make it."

"Michy can't come," Mrs. Peterson said disappointedly. Alan could hear the disappointment in her voice. He knew then that her mother hadn't turned on her. He hoped Mic heard it too.

AJ's curiosity was piqued when he heard his grandmother's voice in the background. "You sound like my mom. Are you my grandma?" he asked the voice in the background.

"Yes I am, AJ. I'm yor Grandma Valerie. I've thought of you ever since yor grandpa mentioned you da oth'r week. It's so wonderful to meet you."

"Grandma, how come you and Grandpa don't like my dad?" His parents didn't see that coming.

"Is that why yor mom can't make it, why da plans have been changed?" she asked.

"No. I said I didn't wanna meet you cause you don't like my dad and you make my mom cry."

His grandma was at a dismay. "AJ, can yor mom hear me?"

"Yes." AJ answered.

"Well, I've nev'r disliked yor dad. I've always thought he was a very charming young man. I've always b'lieved Michy was very blessed to have met 'im. I've sent letters to yor mom askin' her ta forgive her father for da way he acted towards 'im. But I've nev'r r'ceived a reply."

Michelle looked at Alan with a hint of hope. Alan smiled and nodded, encouraging her to say something to her mom. "Mom, I've nev'r r'ceived any letters from you."

"Michy! It's so good to hear yor voice, Baby. I've missed you so much!" She started to cry. "I started writing you after yor first year of marriage. I couldn't find yor phone number. You weren't at da big house anymore. But I knew mail could be forwarded. I just assumed you w're upset with me for not doing more to help you. I'm so sorry, Baby."

"I've missed you too Mom. I thought you had taken Dad's side against me. I've sent you a picture of AJ every year for Mother's Day since da year he was born, but I nev'r heard back from you. I wanted so much for you to be a part of his life. And mine."

"You sent me pictures of AJ!" she said excitedly. "I haven't gotten any," her mom replied. "If neither of us received our letters, where could they be?"

At that moment, a very guilt-ridden Mr. Peterson made a heart-wrenching confession. Hearing his grandson's voice made him want to meet him even more. But hearing his daughter's voice, sounding like her mother, made him realize how much he had missed her also. "They were nev'r mailed," he said. "I took them outta da mail b'fore da postman could get them. And I hid yors from yor mother. I'm so sorry, Michy. This is all my doing. My stubbornness and stupidity has caused us all a lotta unnecessary pain. I've missed you too somethin' awful. And I really wanna meet my grandson. Please forgive me. Please," he pleaded.

They were both hurt once again by the man Michelle had grown up with called Dad. Not only was Mic hurt, but she was livid. The anger towards her dad evident in her reply. "You should be askin' Al that,' Mic told him. "You said some ugly things ta him."

"Mic, that's not necessary," Alan said. "This is about you and AJ."

"Like hell!" Mrs. Peterson said. "It is necessary, Alan. I've missed half of my daughter's life and all of my grandson's because of my husband's foolery and hatred. And now I find out that I have pictures of AJ that I've nev'r seen," she spoke angrily as well. "He had damn well better apologize to all of us. But especially you!" Mr. Peterson didn't say anything. "Go ahead Jeffrey. We're waiting. And it had bett'r sound sincere," she said sternly. Assuming that it wouldn't be.

He made his half-hearted apology to Alan. Everyone could see right through it. But on the brighter side, Michelle had her mother back. They vowed never to be separated again. They were just about to hang up when Mr. Peterson stopped them. "Wait. Don't hang up yet." He went to the credenza and pulled out the huge stack of Val's Mother's Day cards. "These are da cards she sent you."

She hurriedly opened one to see what AJ looked like. She saw Michelle's whole family. "Oh Michy!" she said crying all over again. "Michy, yor family is so beautiful. AJ, yur as handsome as yor dad. I can't wait to meet you in person."

§

Only moments after Alan heard AJ's voice, he awakened out of the coma. Still too weak to speak, he lay quietly listening to his son periodically strike up a conversation with him throughout the morning. Everyone thought that was a good idea, so they all had their one-sided conversation with him; reminiscing their encounter of good times spent with him. As Rob spoke of the early days; for some reason, Alan was reminded of Rebecca and how difficult her sudden death was on everyone. One while, he was sure his friend would never get over that.

§

As happy as Alan was over the next several years enjoying his son, he was still taunted by the pain of his best friend as he watched Rob work his tailbone off trying to mask his heartache. He pretended fairly well in most cases. But Alan knew he was lonely. It wasn't that women weren't interested. It was more like women didn't interest him. Even when they openly flirted with him, he ignored their very existence.

It was early morning and Michelle was preparing for AJ's seventh birthday party. It's a full day of events that will end with his Uncle Rob's unveiling of his birthday gift. They can hardly wait to see AJ's little face when he sees his own amusement park that he can visit any time he wants to at a moment's notice. Until now Alan and Barlow were competing to see who could spoil him the most. When Alan saw the indoor amusement park that took up two of his upstairs room, he laughingly admitted defeat. "I'm not gonna even try to top this," he told Rob. "Now I know why you didn't tell me what you w're doin'. You know this is too much. He's only seven, Rob. The game room alone would have been more than enough. But rock climbing, movie theater with reclining seats and then bumper cars? What w're you thinkin'?"

Barlow patiently listened to Al pretend to be objective of AJ's birthday gift. When he finished pretendedly complaining, Barlow asked, "So, does that mean you don't wanna give da bump'r cars a test run?"

Al's Chester Cat grin immediately surfaced. "Well, if my son's gonna drive, I need to know da vehicle's safe," Al responded. "I got da red one!" he yelled, jumping into the tiny car.

"I look bett'r in black anyway," Barlow replied.

Mic and Ethel heard bells and buzzers, loud voices and laughing coming from upstairs, so they went to see what was going on. There was no way Michelle was going to let this picture-perfect moment of two overly grown men beating each other up in miniature cars get by her. She quickly grabbed her camera and snapped more than a few pictures. Afterwards, she enlightened them, "Y'all know y'all look ridiculous, don't ya?"

Alan emerged from the arena bragging about beating Rob in his own house. "You made it just in time to see me whoop 'im like I caught 'im with my wife."

"Don't tell 'im I let 'im win. That'll be our little secret," Barlow pretended to whisper to Mic, but said it loud enough for Al to hear.

"Now I know who da park is really for," Mic said. "Hopefully y'all will let 'im play up h're once in a while."

"When he's old enough," Alan said jokingly.

"I can't wait to see AJ's face when Rob reveals it to 'im." Michelle said smiling.

"Yeah. It's a shame we're not havin' any more babies," Alan said.

Mic asked grinning, "Why is that?"

"Cause we're gonna have plenty of time for makin' 'em with AJ playin ov'r at Rob's house all da time. I don't think Rob knows what he's gotten 'imself into."

"Nothin' me and my nephew can't handle t'gether. You best b'lieve I've got this." he told them.

The bumper cars were the delight of the party. Parents and seven-year-olds alike couldn't get their fill of them. Mic and Alan had to promise to bring AJ back first thing in the morning just to get him to go home. He would've slept in the bumper car if he could have. The three of them spent lots of down time at the in-house retreat that also housed an observatory for stargazing.

That night, before bed, Michelle noticed Alan in a distant state. She couldn't imagine what could be wrong after such a wonderful day. When she first asked, he tried to pretend nothing was bothering him. But she knows her husband all too well. "You can lie to somebody who will b'lieve ya. You look like yur a hundred miles away from h're. What's wrong?"

"Nothin'. Naw I'm good," he answered.

"Then I guess you left yor heart at Rob's house," she said, letting him know he wasn't fooling her.

He finally confessed, "He's amazin'. He's been amazin' ever since I've known 'im."

"Yes he is," Michelle agreed, "but that's not tellin' me what's botherin' you."

"Puttin' that mini park in his house for AJ," he paused, looking heartbroken at Michelle, "he should be doin' stuff like that for his own son. I don't understand why he won't move on and be happy. I mean, I'd be da first to agree that Becky was one of a kind. But that doesn't mean that there aren't oth'r wonderful women out there. I don't know how to help 'im get past this. I want 'im ta be as happy as I am."

Not knowing what to say for encouragement, because she had shared his exact same sentiments herself, she simply agreed with her husband, "I do too, Baby. I do too." Then she showed him an article in a magazine she was pondering on talking to him about. "Look at this," she said.

"Most Successful Eligible Bachelor Contest." Al read.

"Rob could win that, hands down, with all that he's accomplished for 'imself."

"Yeah but Rob's not interested in meetin' anyone. Rememb'r?" Al argued.

"That's because he hasn't met anyone interestin' enough yet. This is bound to bring some bett'r prospects outta da woodworks." Alan wasn't completely sold. "Come on, Al. It couldn't hurt ta try. If it doesn't work. No harm done. Right?" she argued.

"Okay," he finally said. But he can't know it was us who nominated him.

§

Alan smiled within himself at the memories of him and his family enjoying themselves. The yearning to join the conversation grow stronger with each loving memory. He struggled harder to speak as the memories they spoke of bounce around in his head.

Rob spoke of the first day they met when Ol Smoky the cat got the best of him; knocking him out of the tree. Michelle talked about Rob burning up the food during his first bar-b-que at Chasidy's Little House. Chasidy demanded an apology from Alan for deeming her husband *'too old to enjoy her'* at their engagement dinner. The four beautiful babies they now shared was evidence that he enjoys her fully. When Alan heard Chasidy speaking about the children he had hoped for years that Rob would someday have, he immediately stepped back in time to when he first met Chasidy. And how happy he was for his friend that he had finally found someone special.

§

Barlow had taken a month's leave from work in early February much to everyone's surprise. It was during that time that he met Chasidy and was spending most of this time getting to know her. He was visiting with Chasidy at her home in Cool River Springs when he received a call from Alan about a problem that had arisen at one of the sites that needed his immediate attention. Bringing Chasidy along for the ride; it was the first time they had ventured out in public together. He never even mentioned to Alan that he was seeing someone.

She was sitting in a chair in the corner of Rob's office when Alan walked in with his radar homed directly in on Barlow. Never expecting anyone to be sitting in the corner. "First off, Rob, there's no way any of us could've seen this comin'," he defended.

"How'd we find out about it?" Barlow asked him.

"Da supplier sent out a d'fective product notice."

"Whatta they doin' about it?"

"R'placement beams have already been shipped."

Barlow stared a disapproving stare at Alan. "It's gon set us back two maybe three months ta replace all those beams Al," a frustrated Rob said. "I can't take that back ta Mosaic."

"That's all we've got right now," Alan concluded.

A frustrated Barlow sighed. "Let's go take a look."

It wasn't until that moment when Barlow stood to reach for Chasidy's hand that Alan noticed her. "I'm sorry Mam. I didn't see you sittin' there." Barlow introduced them just ahead of them going out to inspect the defective beams. The introduction was accompanied by the biggest boyish grin Alan had ever seen on Barlow's face. Since the early years that is, with Becky.

"Al, meet Ms Chasidy Weems. Ms Weems, Alan Ferguson. My chief engineer and my best friend."

Alan couldn't wait to share the news with Michelle. Later that day after an emergency meeting with the company, he called her. He now, had his silly Chester Cat grin plastered to his own face. "Bae, put dinn'r in da fridge. We're goin out'. Rob's in town. Have we got a surprise for you!"

"What is it?" Michelle was anxious to know.

"Un unk. You gotta see this to b'lieve it. I'm on my way."

He told Barlow he would pick them up at the hotel after he grabbed Mic from the house. When they got there Mic immediately showered Rob with kisses. Alan saw Chasidy emerge from the bedroom and began scratching his head. "Ugh, Mic. You might wanna stop kissin' all ov'r that woman's husband."

"Husband. What husband? What woman?"

"This husband," he said before physically turning her body to see Chasidy standing in the doorway. "That woman."

Michelle immediately began to protest in her comical high pitch twang, "Rob Barlow. Have you been cheatin' on me?" Without giving him a chance to answer, she said, "It's about doggone time!" She rushed over to Chasidy and grabbed her hand, bringing her to stand directly in front of Rob.

"Mister. You got some serious explaining to do," she said holding Chasidy with one hand and pointing at her with the other one.

Barlow was drowning in laughter at his comical friend. He rescued Chasidy from her clutches, pulling her gently to him and said, "Mic, this is Chasidy. Chasidy, this is Mic. My best friend's wife. And my good friend as well."

"Chasidy, I am so, so glad to meet you. Cause this man is too doggone fine ta be wasting away like a hermit." Michelle wiped her forehead like she was wiping sweat away. "Girl! Now maybe I can have my husband back," she joked. By now Alan had joined Barlow in laughing. "Fair warning, Girl. They've got this weird bromance b'tween 'em that's been going on since they were kids. Get o'er that right now." She said smiling.

"Y'all ready?" Alan asked shaking his head at his wife.

Alan and Mic wanted to hear all about Chasidy and how she and Barlow met. But Barlow and Chasidy hadn't learned how to socialize together yet. They spent most of the evening drifting into zones where there was only the two of them. When Alan was finally able to get his lovesick friend's attention, he made a suggestion that was obviously already in the making, "Rob, why don't you marry da woman? Everybody can see yur in love." A fact that was proven when rob took him at his advice, pulled out a beautiful diamond cluster ring, and proposed right there in front of them.

While Alan was smiling within himself, his voice miraculously returned to him. He relayed a message to Chasidy through AJ in a whisper so soft that no one could hear but him. "Aunt Chasidy."

"Yeah Baby."

"Dad said he apologizes." AJ told her.

"What?" Chasidy asked in surprise.

"Dad said he apologizes and stop talkin' about 'im like he's not here."

He had gotten everyone's attention. All eyes were on Alan. He didn't move. And his eyes were still closed. But the grin plastered to AJ's face told them that he was telling the truth.

Michelle however, wanted proof. She listened for Alan to speak again. When he didn't, she scolded her son, "Boy, you'd bett'r not be playin' with me!"

Alan has always deemed it his responsibility to run interference between AJ and Michelle. This moment was no different. "He is playin' with you. But I did say that." He spoke softly.

Michelle shrieked with joy, rushing to call the nurse, and showering him with kisses.

"Yes, do you need something?" the nurse asked.

"He's awake! He's awake! Al is awake!" she said excitedly.

When the nurse approached the bed, Alan's eyes were still closed. He wasn't moving. The nurse hesitantly asked, "Mr. Ferguson, can you hear me?" Alan didn't answer. She asked him again. He still didn't answer. "Are you sure he was awake?" she finally asked Michelle.

"Yes", Michelle answered. "We all heard 'im."

"Well, he doesn't seem to be awake now." The nurse said looking around the room at everyone.

Michelle knew that even just moments out of a coma, her husband was back to being his usual prankful self again. "Al, if you don't say somethin' ta this woman, I'm gonna have Rob make you walk home."

"And I'll do it too, for makin' us all look like we're crazy," Barlow agreed.

The nurse was thinking they were all probably imagining things. She didn't see any difference in Alan from the last time she checked up on him. That's why he startled her when he said, "They're all crazy. I didn't say a word." AJ bellowed a joyous laugh. And the nurse was relieved that she wasn't surrounded by a bunch of lunatics. She performed a few instructional tests on him to find out his limitations. Then informed him that his doctor would visit him as soon as he arrived on his shift.

Alan had enjoyed listening to his family embrace him. He raised his hand closest to Michelle asking for hers. She placed her hand in his. "I've missed you Mic," he said to her. And then to AJ, "And you too, Little Guy."

AJ didn't give Michelle a chance to answer, "We missed you too Dad. Me and Mom and Uncle Rob and Aunt Chasidy, Cait, and Sam. Even Grandma Val is here."

"And Grandpa Jeff," Michelle added.

"And Grandpa Jeff," AJ repeated.

"I think that about sums it up," Michelle agreed. And then everyone else.

10

SEPARATION ANXIETY

That night after everyone had gone back to their hotel rooms, Mic sat quietly with her head resting on Alan's chest. He caressed her hair as she lay there, thinking how not so long ago, he was at her side when she was hospitalized after the kidnapping. It was one of the worst times of their lives. At one point he thought he might lose her. He was sure she had felt that same anxiety herself over the past few days. "I'm sorry Mic," he said.

"For what?" she asked raising her head.

"For puttin' you through this. Rob tried to get me to take da plane...."

"You stop right there," she scolded. "If we had flown and da plane crashed, we all would've died." She reasoned. "I don't know what I would've done had I lost you, but I wouldn't have had this any oth'r way. You drove b'cause you enjoy drivin'. That's what you've been doin' ev'r since we've been t'gether. AJ and I wouldn't take anythin' for our road trips with you."

"I feel da same way Baby," he agreed. "It hasn't been da same since AJ's been in his new school. I've miss y'all bein' with me. That's why I was so happy when you said you wanted ta come with me."

"We've missed being with you, too. That's why I asked ta come. AJ even brings it up once in a while. But he loves that school so much. We w're glad we had this opportunity," she shared.

"It's settled then," he said, "we'll have to break in da motorhome for sure. Have you been thinkin' about where you wanna go?"

"I haven't come up with anything, but AJ already has some ideas," she said smiling.

"Oh yeah. Where?" Alan asked.

"Da two biggest holes in America," she said with a slightly raised twang. "Niagara Falls and Da Grand Canyon. That kid is determined to give me a nervous breakdown. All that water and rocks and deepness! We're gonna have ta tie 'im to a very short heavy-duty rope." she laughed.

"Yeah I can see 'im leanin' ov'r tryin' ta see how far down they go. But I like that he's becomin' one with nature. They'll be first on da list," Alan promised her.

"Fine with me. But right now, you get some rest," Mic suggested. "I'm kinda tired myself."

"Well, I can rest," he said. "But you can't until you let go of my hand."

"Alan, I don't ev'r wanna let go of yor hand again."

"I'm not goin' anywhere, Mic. I'm not ready to leave you and AJ just yet. Go get some rest Sweetheart."

Dr. Pelonoski scheduled him for x-rays early the next morning to rule out certain possibilities to his limited facial movements. Rob was there early so that he wouldn't miss the doctor. Just before he left for his x-rays, Rob's phone rang. "I think you have an admirer. This is Terrence. This is da second time he's called." He told Alan before he answered. "Terrence! Good mornin'. Yur up awful early, Son."

"Good mornin'. That's what work do for ya. I hope I didn't wake you. Cait told me Uncle Al was outta da coma now." Terrence said.

"Yes, he is. I've got cha on speak'r. He's lis'nin' right at ya. He can't talk very loud or very long. But you can say as much as you want to him."

"I'm not gonna hold you guys. I just want 'im ta know I'm glad he's back with us. Things would be kinda boring without cha Unc."

"Everyone agrees with ya on that, Son. Lis'en Al says thanks for checkin' on im. They're fixin' ta roll 'im down to x-ray."

"Okay, Dad. Lat'r."

While he was out of the room, Rob and Mic talked about living arrangements. "You mentioned going home yesterday. Have ya thought about that much when da time comes?"

"Rob, I've thought about nothin' but that," she said in an uncertain tone.

"Sounds like you need to talk about it," he noticed.

"It's so close to Christmas," she started. "If he gets released before Christmas, ..." she paused. "We could go to his temporary parents I suppose. Who by-da-way, I haven't been able to call. They got new numbers, and I never saved them in my phone."

"I'll see if AJ knows them." He said. "I suppose yor folks are outta da question."

Michelle thought about her parents. She would love to spend Christmas with her mom, but she just didn't trust her dad around Alan. "Rob, can I share somethin' with you?"

"Always."

"I never told anyone this. Not even Al." Barlow became concerned. "When my dad sent me away from Alan when we were kids, the reason I never tried to contact Al is because my dad threatened me. He said if I tried to contact him or even just asked about 'im, he would make sure Al was put away for da rest of his life. And that he would conjure up somethin' if he had to. I don't trust 'im around Alan. Is that a horrible thing to say about my dad?"

"After all he's put you through, absolutely not."

"Last Christmas was da first Christmas he'd spent away from you. He tried to pretend like it didn't both'r him. Like AJ and I and da Marshalls w're enough. Even they noticed he was different without you around. Seriously close to separation anxiety. Let's face it Rob. There's a place in his heart that no one can fill except you."

"For da record, I have a matchin' place in my heart for him. Tell me yor thoughts," he encouraged.

"I'd hate to intrude on Chasidy and da babies. But maybe, just until da holidays are ov'r, we could bunk with you guys?" she pleaded.

"First of all, if you think you would be intrudin' on Chasidy, you don't know her as well as you think you do. What's that word she uses 'Nonsense'. She would love havin' you guys there. In fact, she's probably already had that very thought. You guys can stay as long as you need to. Secondly. I believe he will be home in time for Christmas." That made Michelle smile. "We'll all talk about it when Chasidy gets h're.

Mr. Peterson had been coming to a slow boil watching scenes between Michelle and her family play out every day. For some unexplainable reason, he was developing a unique hatred for Barlow, aside from the one he already had for Alan; that he was doing a poor job of hiding. He walked up just as Barlow and Mic began to talk about them staying for Christmas and listened just outside the door. He became furious and walked a short way down the hall. Mrs. Peterson tried to convince him of how ridiculous he was being. Then they returned and entered the room very shortly after Alan returned from x-ray. Mr. Peterson addressed Barlow before even speaking to anyone, "Did you sleep h're last night?"

Alan didn't care for the tone he used with his friend. Neither did Michelle. "Good mornin' ta you too, Dad," she said before Rob could answer him. She had been paying attention to the tension building between them. She knew Rob wouldn't let that go on for much longer after what she had just told him. Especially if it was upsetting to Alan. It wasn't only upsetting to Alan, but to all of them.

Alan had been talking quite a bit that morning. Barlow wanted him to be alert when AJ got there. "Why don't you get some rest, Buddy. AJ and Chasidy will be h're by lunchtime." Alan didn't need to be told twice. A simple thing like talking took a lot out of him. He encouraged Michelle to get some rest too. She felt compelled to watch over Barlow and her dad. She pleadingly stared at him and her mother. She really was tired.

Rob knew what she was thinking. He was pleasantly surprised that her mother knew also. "Get some rest, Michy. I'll put a muzzle on yor dad's mouth." Michelle chuckled at that. Mr. Peterson, however, didn't think it was funny.

Dr. Pelonoski had already come and gone by the time Chasidy made it there with AJ. She was a little disappointed when she found out she had missed him. "What time will da doctor be in?"

"He's already been h're," Mic answered.

"Good news then?" she asked.

"Well, he doesn't need surgery. That's good news," Mic told her..

"Why do I feel a 'but' coman'?" Chasidy anticipated.

Rob explained. "That is good news. Doctor believes changing da brace will be da solution. He says there's nothin' else he can really do. He's talkin' about sendin' 'im home."

"That sounds good to me," Chasidy spoke carefully.

"Yeah, I think so," Rob agreed. "We'll fly out in a day or two. Mic will go with us to get da house ready for 'im. Let me know what room she wants his equipment in. Then we'll come back and get 'im."

"You mean which room in our house, right?" Chasidy asked for clarification.

"No." Rob purposely manipulated his conversation with Chasidy. "Mic doesn't wanna intrude on you and da babies at Christmas."

Chasidy looked at Mic disapprovingly and then back at Rob. "What did you tell 'er?" she asked on the verge of being upset.

"I said ok," he lied. The Petersons were listening attentively. Mrs. Peterson became confused. She didn't remember the conversation going that way.

"Nonsense!" Chasidy squealed. "Has everybody lost their minds? Well, da real adults h're have already talked about this, right AJ?"

"Yes Mam," he answered.

"Would you kindly tell everyone where we're all going when we leave h're?"

Aunt Chasidy said I would starve cause da only thing Mom can do with a broken collarbone is sit around and look at Dad all day. And that isn't very fair ta Dad cause all he can see is da back of his eyelids. So, we're all going to her and Uncle Rob's until we're all bett'r."

Al said, "I'm crackin' up ov'r that eyelid comment."

"I thought you might appreciate that," she joked and then scolded her husband. "Rob, I'm surprised at you."

"Don't be," Mic came to his defense. "He's just showin' his butt, proving to everybody how well he knows his wife. And for clarification girl, how is sittin' around starin' at my husband all day a bad thing?"

"I'm smilin' at that too, Baby. Can you feel it?" Alan told Mic.

She gave him a soft kiss on the lips. "Yes, I can," she replied.

Mr. Peterson's temperature raised a point with every word they spoke. His jealously had completely overtaken him. When he heard Chasidy demand that they come home with them, he had literally heard enough. "Now, hold on h're. Michy, you promised yor mother a visit for Christmas," he protested.

"Jeffrey," Mrs. Peterson interrupted, "that was before Alan was hurt. I'm sure they wanna be home where Alan can be comfortable."

"You stay outta this, Val. I've been watchin' this whole mess since we first got h're. And it seems Michy and Alan don't make a move unless this Kingpin gives his ok on it. Like his word is law around h're. And now his Mrs. Kingpin is tellin' Michy where ta spend 'er Christmas like she doesn't have da good sense to decide for 'erself."

"Jeffrey! Stop it!" Mrs. Peterson demanded. "This is Michy's decision. You w're h're when she asked Mr. Barlow about staying with them. You w're ease dropping outside da door." Mrs. Peterson told off on him.

"No way, Val! Michy promised you a visit and I'm not gonna let 'er weasel out of it. We're her family. Not this Kingpin and his Mrs. Kingpin."

Rob interrupted him, "Do you really think Mic is gonna leave her family at Christmas or any other time to come stay with you? Cause as you can see for ya' self, AJ's not leavin' his dad's side for anyone." Rob spoke very calmly. "And there's no way I'd let Al go anywhere with you, knowing how you feel about 'im." Michelle was afraid he was going to tell her secret.

Mrs. Peterson could see her husband was upsetting everyone. She knew neither Michelle nor Barlow wouldn't put up with that for much longer. "She tried once more to calm her husband. "Jeffrey, that's enough! You need to stop right now."

As loud as Mr. Peterson was talking, Barlow could still here his friend's whisper plea. He had had enough of Mr. Peterson's foolery also. He was sure he was upsetting Mic and AJ along with everyone else. He needed Barlow to put a stop to it. "Rob."

Rob tried to extend him a less embarrassing exit by excusing his family out of the room. "AJ, why don't you and yor mom go introduce yor grandma to Remi."

"But Uncle Rob, I wanna stay with Dad," AJ pleaded in near tears.

"I've got ya dad. You go ahead." Rob comforted.

"Come on Little Guy," Mic said to him and then her mom, "come on Mom.

"You stay right here Val! Barlow may have his little cult thing going on h're. But yur not part of it. Yur my wife. You do what I say, not him."

"Yur right Mr. Peterson. I was just tryin' ta spare you da embarrassment of them seein' you being escorted outta h're. But we'll do it yor way. Al gave you a chance to make things right with yor daught'r and get to know yor grandson. You've manage ta screw that up by being a complete jack. How all of that turned into sheer hatred for me, I don't know. Quite frankly, I don't care. What I do know is yur upsettin' my family. I won't have that. It stops now or I'll have you escorted outta h're."

"You can't make me leave Barlow. This is my daughter's room. If anybody's gonna leave, it's gonna be you and yor kingpin wife h're."

"Mr. Peterson, I not only can, but will," Rob stood to call for hospital personnel.

"Rob. Don't." Mic told him.

"See Barlow. Blood is thicker than water." Mr. Peterson was so blinded by his jealousy and hatred of Barlow and Al that he couldn't see that his own daughter was about to have him thrown out also.

She gently squeezed Al's hand for support. "Alan is my husband," she said. "If anybody is gonna throw anybody out..."

Mrs. Peterson interrupted. She refused to let her daughter fall victim to her husband's foolery. "Jeffrey. Leave," she said.

"Mom!" Mic protested.

"Michy, I couldn't let you do it. It would've laid on yor heart for a long time. Yur just not made that way. I won't have you gettin' sick again because of yor father."

"Sick?" Mr. Peterson asked.

"Yeah Jeffrey. When you kept her from me, it put a strain on her heart. Now she has a heart condition. I'm not gonna let you kill my daughter."

"Michy?" He stared remorsefully at his daughter. "You didn't tell me."

"On purpose."

Mr. Peterson calmed down after learning about Michelle's heart. "And whatta you gonna do?" he asked his wife.

She put her arms around Mic and AJ. "My family needs me. I'm gonna go with them to help Mrs. Barlow take care of them if Mr. Barlow has room on his plane for one more. She can't take care of them and four brand new babies too."

"Well, what am I supposed to do?" Mr. Peterson asked.

"I don't know. But you'll have plenty of quiet time to figure that out. In da meantime, you can go waddle in yor misery alone."

Alan imagined how Mic and AJ must be feeling. He remembered the day on Rob's porch when they decided together to invite her parents into AJ's life. If he had known it would cause them this kind of pain... But that's something he couldn't have possibly known. "Little Guy," he called for his son. AJ moved closer to him. "Mic." She leaned closer to him also. "I'm so sorry. I nev'r meant to hurt eith'r of you. I thought I was doin' da right thang by you and AJ. I just wanted...."

"Shhh," Mic said. "You did a wonderful thing, Al. I have my mom back. And AJ has his grandmoth'r. I'll nev'r understand my dad's animosity t'wards you. But that's his problem. Not ours."

"She's right, Son," Mrs. Peterson agreed. I am so happy Jeffery didn't come between da two of you. I knew you w're meant to be togeth'r when I saw you in da café when you w're just teenagers. Both of you looked so happy. But Michy, she's never looked as happy at home as she looked with you that day. And lat'r on when I would see you around town, you looked so sad." She looked at Michelle. "He never once looked at another girl the whole time you were away. I wanted to tell you, but I didn't want you to hate yor father." She put her hand on top of Michelle's hand holding on to Alan's. "Don't second guess yorself, son. You did everything right."

"Thank you Mrs. Peterson," Al said.

"One more thing, young man."

"What's that?" he asked.

"I'm Mom. Not Mrs. Peterson."

"Yes Mam..... Mom."

#

Two days before he was scheduled to be discharged, Michelle noticed Alan restless in his sleep. It got so intense one night, she decided to wake him. Or so she thought. "Al. Al wake up."

"I am awake," he answered.

"What's wrong, Baby? It looks like yur havin' a nightmare."

"What hap'ened ta da people who hit us?" he asked her.

"I don't know. Da last Rob told me was that da young lady was in surgery. She was pregnant. She had her two-year old son with her who miraculously came out without a scratch. Why do you ask?"

"I was just wonderin' if there's anythang I can do to help 'em. This wasn't their fault eith'r, ya know. I'd hate to get home and find out lat'r there's somethin' I could've done ta help but didn't."

When Rob walked in on the conversation, he explained that the young lady had since died, and the babies were orphaned.

Alan has never cared for the word, orphan. He felt compelled to correct that. "Mic, I won't have those babies all alone. Not at Christmas."

"Are you sayin' you wanna take them with us for Christmas?" she asked.

"Yes," he said at first. "No. I wanna take 'em with us permanently." She became quiet. He sensed something in her quietness. "Mic, you know my history. You know how I've always felt about being an orphan. I won't

173

have those kids go through life alone. Possibly separated."

Michelle was concerned about that. "I'll tell ya what. You sleep on it overnight. And if you still feel da same way in da mornin', I'll see what I can find out about bringin 'em with us." But after they both slept on it overnight and Alan hadn't changed his mind, she couldn't come up with a single reason why they shouldn't take the children with them. When Michelle agreed, Barlow promised he would look into getting the children for them.

11

A CHRISTMAS FOR AL

Alan and Michelle came home to the Barlows looking forward to one of the best Christmases they had ever had. Alan's genuine ability to laugh at adversity and accentuate the positive over the years had somehow rolled over into Mic's spirit. As far as they were concerned being wrapped in bandages gave them more reasons to expect to see Christmas Miracles. Alan's hope never dwindled. Neither did Mic's. She had her mom with her. It was their first Christmas together in over twenty-five years. And that meant everything to her. Alan could hear the joy in her voice each time she spoke. Hearing his wife and child enjoying their time together with his mother-in-law was priceless. That meant everything to him.

Alan's senses were working overtime. The house smelled like evergreen and cinnamon. He tried to envision what Chasidy had done to the place. When Mic opened the door to check on him, she noticed him in a state of serenity. She just stood and stared at him for a moment. She was startled when he spoke. "Why are you standin' there. Come on ov'r."

"Hey. Don't you be getting used to these extra special senses you've got going on h're. I miss those handsome ambers."

"They miss you plenty too."

"You looked so peaceful just now. What w're you thinkin' about?" Mic asked.

"Da house smells so festive. I was just imaginin' what Chasidy has done to da place," he answered.

"Nothin'," Mic said.

Al was shocked by that. "Nothin'?"

"Not a thing. Mom wouldn't let 'er. Chasidy just pointed her in da direction of da decorations. Mom took it from there. AJ and I helped a little. But Mom wouldn't really let any of us do very much. You should've seen her. She really enjoyed 'erself."

"That's great," Al replied. "I'm imaginin' evergreen garland everywhere. Over da fireplace and da doorways, all accented with red and gold poinsettias."

"How--- do you do that? Are you sure you can't see?" Mic asked him in amazement.

"Even if I could, I haven't been outta this room since I've been h're."

"That's right, you haven't," she admitted.

"What else has she done?"

"Da tree is amazin! Chasidy's tree is white with only gold decorations. That... is so my mom's touch. Each room had its own color theme. It brings back so many memories, Al."

Michelle was never able to talk about her mom before because of the pain it caused her. Alan wanted to keep her basking in the memories. "Tell me about them." They were interrupted by a knock at the door. It was Mrs. Peterson and AJ.

"I thought you might like some hot chocolate," she said, "ta get that soupy taste outta yor mouth. You've gotta be tired of that stuff."

"Thanks. Hot chocolate sounds good," Al told her.

"This is perfect," Mic said. "I was just about ta tell Al about Christmas at home."

Mrs. Peterson looked at AJ smiling, "We made it just in time, didn't we?"

"Almost perfect," Al corrected.

Michelle already knew what would fix that. She grabbed her phone and called Rob to invite him and Chasidy to the party. Mrs. Peterson grabbed two more mugs from the kitchen. This was the first time any of them heard Michelle speak of her childhood. She and her mom reminisced together. It was evident that she and her mom had always been close.

Mrs. Peterson told how Mic loved making gingerbread houses. "I remember da last one we made togeth'r. Do you rememb'r, Sweetheart?"

"Yes, I do," Mic answered.

"It was an entire gingerbread scene with da house, da dad, mom, a little girl, and a little boy. We had so much fun putting that thing togeth'r."

"Yeah, when we finished, I didn't wanna eat it cause I didn't wanna mess it up." Mic said.

"I'll bet. You put a lotta work into it," Rob said. "That must've been a big accomplishment for a little girl.

"It was a lotta work." Mrs. Peterson shared. "We worked most of da day on it. She was so meticulous."

"That's a long time for a six or seven-year-old child to work on somethan'," Chasidy said. "I couldn't find anythang that held Caitlin's attention for most of da day. Except cartoons." She chuckled.

"Six or seven?" her mom repeated, laughing a little herself. Michy was much older than that."

"Mom." Mic protested. "No, I wasn't."

"So how old was she, Mrs. Peterson?" Chasidy asked.

"That was da Fall I had seen Michy with her friends at the café. She was sitting next to Al having da time of her life. She called the house a castle. And the man and woman were the da Prince and Cinderella. Da kids were their children. She had built her dream life with Alan out of gingerbread, and she couldn't bear to ruin it. She was fifteen years old."

"Mom, you knew about Al even back then?" Mrs. Peterson just smiled.

"Did you guys ever wonder why out of da blue you could order anything you wanted and never had to pay for any of it?"

"I wondered about that quite often," Rob admitted. "I even asked Sanderford if he had anythin' ta do with it." He started laughing. "So, it was you?"

"I've always wanted you to be happy Michy. Every now and then I would sneak in on you guys just to watch you enjoy yorself."

"Mom." Michelle started to cry.

"So, what did y'all do with da house?" Chasidy asked.

"We loaded it up and took it to da children's shelter."

'It's no wonder she missed her mom so much,' Alan thought. "Sounds like Christmas was a special time in da Peterson's home," he said.

"Al. Every day with Michy was special with me."

"I'm glad yur h're with us Mom," he added, "with Mic."

"Me too, Grandma!" AJ said excitedly.

Barlow and Chasidy were so happy for Michelle. They hated to leave, but it was time for quad patrol.

"Sounds like it's time for us to say goodnight. Duty calls," Barlow told them when one of the babies began to cry.

"AJ and I are gonna call it a night too," Mic's mom said. "I've enjoyed this Michy. I love you, Baby. Goodnight."

"Love you too Mom. Goodnight."

AJ hugged his dad and kissed his mom. But he took a minute to gaze upon his mother's face. "What is it, Little Guy?" she asked him.

"You look beautiful, Mom," he said. "You look happy. I like that."

"Thank you Little Guy," she said smiling. "Now get outta h're b'fore you make me cry."

"Good night Mom. Good night Dad."

"Good night Little Guy," they said.

"Mic, has he ev'r done that b'fore?" Al asked once he was gone.

"Nev'r," Mic answered gleaming.

"Wow, that makes me wanna see yor beautiful face all da more right now."

"If y'all don't stop. Yur gonna make me blush," she said.

"And I'd love to see that too," he added.

#

The next day Mic was telling Chasidy how adorable AJ was last night.

"Well, girl, like I shared with yor husband a short while ago; he may be senselessly in love with his dad, but he's plenty crazy about his mom too. He protected you somethan' fierce in da hospital."

"I know. Y'all told me. I feel so bad for deserting 'im. Have you seen 'im, by da way?"

"I think he's with Rob. They may be shop'pan." Chasidy answered. "So, have y'all decided on a name for Baby Jane?" Chasidy asked. That question got Mic's juices flowing. She has quietly become very excited about her new future family members.

"We're thinkin' maybe Lois Grace. I like Lois but Alan's stuck on Grace. He says it's by God's Grace that they're alive. That we're all still alive. But Alan would really like ta name 'er after her mother. But we don't know what that is." Mic explained.

Chasidy called Rob to see if he knew the mother's name. When she hung up the phone, she spoke one word, "Katherine."

"Katherine. That's beautiful. With a 'C' like her broth'r. I'm gonna go tell Al right now." She hurried off to Al's bedroom.

"Slow down!" Chasidy yelled to her. "Yur fresh outta collarbones!"

When she entered the room, Al immediately began talking, "My son has d'serted me."

"He's out shoppin' with Rob. But this should cheer ya up. Catherine Grace."

"What hap'ened with Lois?"

"Baby Jane's mom's name is Katherine."

"It is? What else do we know about 'er?" he asked as excitedly as he could.

"Nothin'. You don't want Rob ta do all da work for you, do ya?"

"Yur right. This is my quest."

"Ugh. Wrong." Mic corrected. "This is our quest."

#

While AJ and his Uncle Rob shopped, he bought his dad a new phone to replace the one that was lost in the accident. When they returned from shopping, he and Rob began wrapping their gifts. His dad's phone had only finished charging fifteen minutes when it rang and startled AJ. Barlow laughed. "Should I answer it, Uncle Rob?"

"How else are you gonna know who it is?" Rob answered. "B'sides, it might be business."

"Hello."

"AJ,… is that you?" the voice asked.

"Mama Kelly?" he asked in return.

"Oh Baby, I'm so glad I was able to reach you. We've been worried sick about all of you."

"Uncle Rob. It's Mama Kelly. They're worried about us." AJ told his uncle.

"Go get yor mom. I'll talk to 'er," Rob said. As Michelle walked up she heard Rob apologizing for not sending them word of Alan's condition. And that he couldn't call because he didn't have her number. "I'll fix that as soon as we hang up," he assured. "Here's Mic now." Then he reached the phone to Michelle. "Mrs. Marshall," he told Michelle.

"Mama Kelly!" Michelle began. "I've wanted to call you, but I didn't have yor number. It was lost with Alan's phone," she explained.

"How is Alan, Dear? We heard about the accident on the news. We wanted to come but we couldn't find out what hospital he was in. We've been so worried."

"Yeah, that hospital is strict about not giving out information. He was in a coma for a while. We're home now though. Well, almost. We're stayin' with Rob. Why don't come see for yorself. Al would love to see ya." Michelle extended an invitation.

"Is it alright with Robert?" she asked.

"You mean, da Robert Al left you for ta live und'r a railroad track just to be near 'im. You really think he's gonna deny 'im that?" Michelle teased.

Rob laughed. "Tell her da more da merrier."

"Did ya hear that?"

"Yes, I did," Mrs. Marshall answered laughing. Mr. Marshall spoke something in the background. "Stan wants to know if we can speak with Alan."

"That would absolutely make his entire Christmas. But it would kinda spoil AJ's Christmas gift to him. This is his new phone. AJ was wrap'in it when it rang." Mic explained.

"Well, we don't wanna ruin his gift," Mrs. Marshall agreed.

"Besides, it would be a nicer surprise seein' you in person," she reiterated.

"Then we'll see you in a couple-a days," she said. "I can't wait to see my boy."

"Our boy," Mr. Marshall corrected.

"Do you need me to send someone for you?" Rob asked them. Michelle relayed the question.

"Why don't you take 'im up on that off'r? It's a long ride," Michelle encouraged.

"We'll be fine," Mr. Marshall said. "Thank ya though. Text me the address. Look for us around noon."

For the next couple of days, the New Little House was as busy as a beehive. Everybody had a special surprise for each other that they could hardly wait to give. And Alan and Michelle wanted to get past Christmas so that they could meet their new family members of whom they were told wouldn't arrive until the day after Christmas.

When Christmas Eve arrived, everyone was ready to relax and get rested for the big day. Mrs. Peterson baked Christmas cookies and made hot cocoa that everyone enjoyed in the bedroom with Alan. When she entered, she declared, "This feels like another hot chocolate moment. But we've got cookies this time to go with it."

Alan, in his usual playful manner complained, "Y'all wrong for eatin' warm cookies in h're and I can't have any."

Michelle bargained with him. "When you lose that brace, I'll bake a whole batch just for you."

"Son, you'll have cookies comin' outta yor ears, cause I'm gonna bake you a batch too," Mrs. Peterson added.

And then Chasidy, "You'll be an official cookie monster with my batch included in that bunch."

"That'll teach you to complain, won't it?" Barlow said laughing. Alan was laughing inside also.

But then Mrs. Peterson said, "You didn't really think I'd leave my favorite son-in-law out, did ya? Try this."

"That smells like gingerbread," he said.

"It is. After our walk down memory lane the other night, I just had to make some for us."

Mic placed a small piece in his mouth. It was so soft, he barely had to chew at all. "I don't know if its Mic's fingers or da cookie, but somethin's delicious."

They all shared a laugh. But Rob made a comment. "Buddy, yur gonna be just fine."

Rob and Chasidy left the family to their fun when the Quad started calling for them. Once feeding time was over, they retired for the evening. When Michelle and AJ started counting the yarns, Mrs. Peterson insisted they all call it a night as well. "Come on Little Guy. Let's let mom and dad get their rest. You could probably use some yorself."

Mic returned from the bathroom ready for bed. "This was a wonderful evenin', AL," Mic said to him. "I wish it didn't have to end."

"Come h're," he said. "Lay b'side me. We can't stop it from ending. But we can stay t'gether t'night."

"Are you sure it won't be too uncomfortable?"

"My head can't move, and part of my face doesn't work. But my arms are still strong enough to hold my lovely wife as long as I want."

"That's what I'm talkin' about," a very happy Mic replied while climbing into bed with Al.

Christmas Day had finally arrived. There were so many hopeful Christmas Miracles imagined for the blessed day. Everyone in the house had one or two tucked away in his or her heart. And the Lord had no intentions of disappointing them. Rob and Chasidy were in the kitchen finishing up breakfast and AJ had just taken a bite out of his bacon when they heard Michelle shriek. Everyone ran in to see what was wrong. They found Michelle leaning over Alan in tears. Neither of them could see Alan. "Mom, what's wrong with Dad?" AJ asked in near hysterics.

Michelle didn't answer. Rob decided to try. "Mic, what's hap'ened? Is anythin' wrong with Al?" She was so overcome with emotions, she couldn't speak. She beckoned for everyone to come closer without raising her head. When she did, they all shared their own bit of emotions when they saw Alan's eyes wide open looking at them.

"Dad, can you see me?" AJ asked.

"I sure can Little Guy," he answered, "and what a handsome sight you are for my sore eyes." AJ ran to him giving him a huge hug.

"This is da best present ev'r!" AJ told him.

"Tell me that again when you see yor real gift," Al replied.

"You got me something for Christmas?" he asked excitedly.

"Me and yor mom. Yes we did."

"But we all were in da hospital."

"Little Guy," Al said, "we had yor gift months ago."

Every time Michelle was able to stop herself from crying, she started up again each time she looked at Alan's handsome ambers.

"I think we should give 'em a minute," Chasidy said.

"I think we should give 'em somethin' else too," Rob said.

They went next door to Sam's bungalow to retrieve their own Christmas surprise for them. They had secretly brought the babies home with them and decided they would make the perfect Christmas gift. Chasidy opened the door slowly. "Mic, are you done cryin' in h're, Girl?" Chasidy asked.

Michelle began fanning herself. "Yes, I think so," she said. "I reserve da right to start up any time though."

"Ok, well, let me see if I can get you started up again," Chasidy said walking in with little Grace in her arms. Rob was right behind Chasidy with little Charles. "Merry Christmas guys!" He took great pleasure in placing him in Al's lap.

"When did they get h're?" Alan asked.

"Da same day you did," Rob answered. "Chasidy and I wanted to surprise you for Christmas."

"Well, you did that," Alan said. "Thanks Buddy!" Then he said to his son, "AJ, this is yor new brother."

"I know." AJ said. "We've met. I've been playin' with 'im ov'r at Sam's."

"Are these da children from da accident?" Mrs. Peterson asked.

"Yes," Mic answered smiling down at Grace. "Look at 'er Mom. She's beautiful, isn't she?"

"Perfect," Mrs. Peterson answered. "Just perfect. Da both of them."

"We'll leave you all to get acquainted. I'll bring breakfast in to ya. Sunrise Service starts at 6:30," Rob said.

#

Being able to attend church had a whole new meaning for Alan. He has always been grateful for things God has blessed him with. But he keeps reflecting on the accident and how that one incident could have changed all of their lives forever. He knew in his heart it was time to make some serious changes.

He knew Rob was planning to be baptized. Mic shared that with him. He was thinking maybe it was time he and his family did the same.

He listened attentively as the pastor's sermon reminded the congregation of the gift of salvation that came with the birth of Christ. He was familiar with the story, however, today it had a new meaning to him as he was filled with a different kind of joy.

After the service, he was anxious to give AJ his gift. He instructed Sam to take them around back of their house. The car had barely stopped moving when AJ jumped out running to the newly built stables. There were five horses; each one in his own stall with a tag attached. The tags were turned backwards. He had patted every single horse before the others even made it to the stables. When he found himself in front of the beautiful black Friesian, his feet were planted.

"Y'all have ta guess which one is yors," Al told them, "before turning da tags around.

Chasidy zeroed in on the enchanting white appaloosa with black and grey spots. "If my name isn't on this one, we're gonna have to change that."

Barlow walked back and forth between the handsome chestnut German work horse and the gorgeous Chocolate Paint. He finally stopped in front of the work horse fully admiring him. "This looks like me. If not, what Chasidy said."

Mic, who wasn't really into animals, chose the one Rob didn't choose. That left a beautiful white Friesian for Alan to compliment AJ's. They were all smiles when they flipped their tags to find that they had all chosen the correct horses. "I know you guys pretty good, don't I?" Al bragged.

On the way back to the car, AJ walked with his dad. He gave him a hug and made him a solemn promise,

"Thanks Dad. I'm gonna take good care of 'im. I can't wait 'til we can go ridin' t'geth'r."

Alan had done a good thing. And just as they turned the corner to the front of Rob's house, Al saw that Mic had done her own good thing as well by surprising him with a brand-new Silverado equipped with all the latest technology and painted in his absolute favorite color, red. Alan was completely speechless when he saw it and absolutely awestruck with his wife. He lovingly stared at her endlessly until AJ pushed her closer to him and he rendered her a tender hug. Then he reached for his son and hugged him again too.

"Let's get you inside Buddy," Barlow told him, "Before that brace gets too cold and freezes yor face off."

They all laughed. Al wanted to laugh. And Chasidy scolded her husband. "Rob, you just ruined a beautiful kodak moment h're," she said laughing also.

Barlow perched Al in Chasidy's massage chair while they waited for family to arrive just in case he became tired and needed to rest; he wouldn't have to move to the bed. They talked for a spell about the events over the past weeks. Barlow talked about Nurse Tammy and how she was such a big help to them. "I couldn't get anything out of anyone ov'r da phone. Until she showed up and took ov'r da call. She even stayed with AJ until we got there. I'm sorry you didn't get a chance to meet er."

"Why is that?" Al asked.

"That night was her last night b'fore goin' on v'cation. She won't be back until after da first of da year."

"I gotta do somethin' for 'er." Alan vowed. "That'll give me and Mic time to come up with somethin'." He didn't tell Al that he had shown his own appreciation in his own Barlow kind of way. "And speakin' of Mic. Can you believe that truck man? I think she's learning new things from yor wife."

"I think we're all learning new things from my wife," Barlow said. "Those horses are a phenomenal idea. I'm in agreeance with AJ. I can't wait for us all to go ridin' t'geth'r."

"Me too," Al agreed. "We all may be learnin' from her, but you and Chasidy seem to have merged into one mindset. A pearl-colored GMC and a matching Bentley that neither of you knew was comin'. That's awesome." He noticed Barlow drifting away for a second. "Rob, is somethin' wrong?" Just then little Grace started crying. They ladies were busy in the kitchen, so he asked Rob to bring her to him.

After he made sure she was snug in his arms, he proceeded to fix her a bottle. Upon his return, he answered Alan's question. "I'm gonna get baptized. That's why Chasidy and I invited da Pastor ov'r for dinn'r. I'm gonna talk to 'im about it taday."

"That's great Rob. What brought this on though?"

"No one particular thing, I don't think. I'm thinkin' everythin' ov'r da past two years. But especially since da quad was born. I wanna raise 'em in church. Und'r da Grace of God."

"Man. You may not believe me, but I've been thinkin' along those same lines since da accident. I haven't talked ta Mic about it yet though. But I'm really thinkin' it time."

"Maybe you should do that." Rob suggested.

In the kitchen, the ladies heard little Grace crying. Michelle never stopped stirring her pasta. "Mic," Chasidy said. "That's not one of mine. But it might be if one of 'em decides to join 'er." They both went to check on Grace by which time she had stopped crying. They found her peacefully in Al's arms waiting for Rob to bring her bottle.

Alan teased, "Is this yor way of r'mindin' me that I got you into this?"

"No, Honey I'm sorry," Mic apologized. "It's my way of gettin used to having new little people in da family. It won't hap'en again."

"Mic," he said, "calm down. I've got 'er."

Mrs. Peterson giggled as she offered her assistance. "Are you comfortable with her, AL? Do you want me to take 'er?"

"Thanks Mom. I really am good."

While they were talking, Chasidy's family arrived. Chasidy was shocked to see Terrence and his family entering before Caitlin. Even if he's not late, he's certainly never early. But, he had taken a real liking to his Uncle Al. He wanted to see for himself how he was faring. As soon as he walked in; after they all finished making moderation over the new vehicles out front, he made his way straight to Alan with everyone else following suit behind him. "Merry Christmas!" he said to everyone. And then he said to Al with a Merry Christmas grin on his face, "I'm feelin' that fancy headgear, Unc. Is that da new style. I'll bet it's hard to find a tie ta match that."

"Oooh!" Caitlin said. "You are so wrong for that!"

Everybody laughed. Then Barlow said grinning, "That's why he didn't wear one to church taday."

Even Alan laughed a real laugh at that one that sent his face into a painful frenzy. But he deemed that one worth it. "Have you been hangin' out with my jester?" he asked Terrence.

When Michelle saw her husband in total miserable pleasure she happily announced, "Okay. Yur officially his favorite nephew. Y'all might even be blood related."

After that, AJ took the guys to show off his horse. The ladies went to help out in the kitchen. The twins found their way to the new babies. And Rob made his way to the porch to wait for Pastor Bishop while Al and Mic had their talk about getting baptized.

Chasidy heard another car pull up. She joined Rob on the porch to see who it was, hoping it was one of her own surprises. Rob was shocked to see Mr. Peterson drive up. No one knew Chasidy had invited him to be with his wife. He was anxious to see her again. But he first had to right another senseless wrong and so, he came with a sincere apology first to Alan and then to Barlow. "I hope you don't mind my being h're, Mr. Barlow. Yor wife invited me."

"Mic, Mrs. Peterson!" Chasidy yelled.

"What is it, Chasidy?" Mrs. Peterson asked before they both stopped at the door, in shock as well. Mr. Peterson smiled at them both.

"We'll leave you three alone," Rob said.

"Wait, Mr. Barlow," he said. "I'd like to talk to you and my son-in-law first."

"Okay. Follow me." He kissed his wife and Mic on the way by.

He didn't make excuses for his actions. He shared the story, however, of him losing his own son when he was only three. "I wasn't always like this. That changed me tremendously. Val nev'r would've married a man like da one I've b'come. It broke my heart when I heard about Michy's condition. And to know that I was da blame for it. I love my family. And I can see that da two of you love 'em too. I truly apologize for da way I've acted t'wards you two. Especially you Alan. Michy couldn't have made a bett'r choice even if she'd tried." He chuckled. "Which I know for a fact, she didn't. She's nev'r loved anyone else but you. Will you accept my apology please? Both of you? My sincere apology this time."

"Da moment you started talkin', Mr. Peterson," Alan replied.

And then Rob, "What he said."

The moment Mr. Peterson put out the fires between them, AJ received him freely as his grandpa. He saw them hugging when he entered the room and ran to him immediately embracing him. "Grandpa! I didn't know you w're comin'."

"I didn't eith'r, son. It was kind of a last- minute decision," he explained.

Michelle and her mom joined them in the living room with their own acts of affections. But Michelle won't be settled until her husband's last surprise is here. It's already past noon and the Marshalls hadn't arrived yet. She was beginning to think they may not arrive in time for Christmas dinner.

After her father settled in with her mom, she stepped away from the hustle and bustle to call and check up on the Marshalls. When she didn't get an answer, she immediately voiced her concern to Rob. "You don't think somethin' hap'ened to them, do ya?"

"Mic, God protected yor family in a near fatal accident. He miraculously opened Alan's eyes first thing this mornin' so he wouldn't miss a single festivity today. And he brought yor dad with a sincere apology ta Al, here to be with all of you. Do you really believe that aft'r all of that, He's gonna let somethin' hap'en ta Alan's temporary parents?" he reasoned through his faith. "This is clearly a Christmas for Al. They'll be h're." Barlow said without a doubt.

"Thank you," she said kissing him on the cheek.

By the time they had finished talking, the car was coming up the road to the driveway. Mrs. Peterson happen to be closest to the door when they knocked, so she opened it. "Hello."

"Merry Christmas! We're da Marshalls," Mr. Marshall said. Mrs. Peterson didn't know them, even though, they looked vaguely familiar. The Marshalls could tell she was stomped. "We're here to see our son Alan," he explained.

Just then AJ walked up behind Mrs. Peterson. "Who is it, Grandma?" But then he saw for himself. "Papa Stan!" He hurried to hug them both. "Mama Kelly! Dad's gonna be blown away."

By now Rob and Mic had reached the door. "Hey!" Rob spoke as he too reached for hugs. "Come on in outta da cold." Then he turned to Chasidy who had by now made her way to the door as well. "This is my wife Chasidy. Chasidy, da Marshalls. Alan's temporary parents," he said smiling.

"What?" Chasidy asked for clarity.

"Yes, it's true," Mrs. Marshall confirmed. "And it wasn't nearly long enough."

But Mic was anxious to get them to Alan. "Let's make this an after-dinner conversation," she interrupted. "It's too adorable *and long* ta rush through. Come on, I'll take you to Al." She walked with her arm around Mama Kelly. Once again, Alan was taken aback when he saw his temporary parents standing in front of him. They too were in a sad awe when they saw Alan sitting in the chair in such a fragile looking state and Michelle wearing matching bandages to AJ's.

Alan proceeded to stand up to greet them. "Son," Mr. Marshall said, walking towards him. But Mrs. Marshall reached him first when she hurried past her husband and extended him a hug nearly knocking him back into the chair. Mr. Marshall just had to get in where he could. She wasn't letting him go.

"We were so worried." She began to cry. Then she reached for Michelle and AJ. "About all of you. We couldn't reach you."

"My phone was lost in da accident," Alan told her what Mic and Rob had already told her. "I'm so glad you guys are h're."

They stayed there hugging for more than just a few minutes. Until Chasidy and Mrs. Peterson returned to the kitchen to finish preparing dinner. Michelle and Mrs. Marshall then joined them.

Rob heard another car pulling up. He knew that had to be Pastor Bishop, their last guest. Once everyone was present and accounted for, Chasidy semi-formally introduced everyone. "Okay, y'all, let's get everyone acquainted. This is Pastor Bishop. These are da Petersons. Michelle's parents. These are da Marshalls. Alan's parents. They call them temporary. Although I don't know why; cause if they were, they wouldn't be h're taday." She paused to share a confused emoji pose with them. Then continued. "This is Charles. His sistar Grace is in da nursery. They're da newest membars to da Ferguson family. And last but certainly not least, this is my family. My Mom, Rosalee and my children and grandchildren; Caitlin, Antonio, Terrence, Jasmine, McKenna, and McKenzie. Just call em 'Da Gang' until y'all learn everybody's names.

"Alan, Mic. You have more children?" Mrs. Marshall asked.

"That's anoth'r aft'r dinn'r story," Michelle said smiling. "I *really* don't wanna rush that one."

"We've got a lot to catch you up on," Alan added.

There was so much going on the rest of the day, they never had time for those conversations. Barlow and Alan had big announcements to make that they shared with everyone at the dinner table. That was the major subject for the rest of the dinner. "I'm gonna be baptized. I'd like ya all ta be there," Barlow shared.

And then Alan. "So are we, as a family."

The Marshalls weren't the least bit surprised by that. Alan has always followed Barlow everywhere. The Petersons were vastly learning this.

Chasidy immediately left the table and came back with gifts for the both of them. "These w're gonna be for lata'. But I think this is da perfect time." She handed Rob his box and proceeded on to Alan. She gave them both beautiful giant gold-trimmed bibles with a family heritage section in the front and smaller study bibles with commentaries. But Alan had a special extra gift. "I'm learnan' new things from my husband," she started. Then she handed him an envelope. "It's okay ta not know where you come from. You can record yor family heritage starting with da beautiful family you have right now right h're. Or you can opan this envelope and continue da search fa yor past. Eithar way, I think you'll be pleased."

"Thank you Chasidy. I'm so glad we married you." Alan seriously teased.

After dinner they enjoyed a non-traditional gift exchange game of Scavenger Hunt. Everyone pitched in trying to figure out the gifts so that they didn't have to hunt for them. Their motivation being a tired and worn-out Alan who wanted to participate in the festivities but wasn't fully recovered.

Chasidy had clues to help everyone along in the game. However, the clues were too easy. *On purpose.* So, she was constantly extended a friendly reminder; "You should've let Uncle Al and Dad make da clues," by her gang.

She playfully handled her own defense, "For da record, if it weren't for Al needan' to get back to bed soon; this would be a full-scale scavenger hunt. All y'all would've been hun' tan fa yar gifts."

When everybody in the room guessed Terrence's gift was a motorcycle; even Barlow concluded, "Chasidy, everybody knows what that is. You really should've let me, and Al make da clues."

Alan added, "Next year, it's a given. Rob and I have clue duty."

Chasidy had only changed up tradition because Alan was still limited health wise. So, because of that, she posed an obvious question, "Yur not plannan' ta be well by then?"

Alan was completely exhausted by the time the game was over. He had spent hardly any time with his parents. Barlow began to help Mic escort him to his room. "Robert," Mr. Marshall stopped him. "I can do that. If you don't mind."

"Don't mind at all, Sir." Barlow told him.

"Mama, can you come too?" Al asked.

Michelle happily felt like a third wheel. "Why don't I let you enjoy yor parents for a while. Call when yur ready to get settle in."

He didn't talk much. He was just too tired. So, his parents did most of the talking. He just laid there and basked in their company. Before they left he said, "I don't know how Mic pulled this off. But I'm glad she did. This is da best Christmas I've ev'r had. Thank you for comin'." Then he wanted to kiss the babies before falling asleep. "Will you ask Mic to bring da babies please?" He had plenty of assistance with that. Mrs. Marshall barely let them out of her sight once she got a glimpse of them. She and Mrs. Peterson were more than happy to bring them in for him.

He held Grace first staring at her in amazement. Grateful that she's a part of his life. He gently kissed her good night and gave her to Mic. Little Charles instinctively climbed into his dad's arms when they were free. He sat there playing in his dad's lap with one of the toys he received earlier. Then he leaned over and laid on Alan's chest. When Mrs. Peterson tried to take him, he shook his little head. "No," he said.

"No?" Mrs. Peterson repeated.

Then Mrs. Marshall tried to take him. She got the same reaction. When Michelle returned from the nursery after putting Grace in her bassinet, they told her about Charles's resistance to leaving his new dad. Michelle decided she would give it a try. "Come on Charlie. Let daddy go to sleep."

"No," he said a third time, whimpering.

Alan was basking inside. Just as content with his new son as his new son was with him. "It's okay Mic. We can take a nap t'geth'r. Someone can come get 'im after he falls asleep." As it turned out even after Charles fell asleep, no one was able to take him from Alan's arms. "If Mic wasn't such fierce competition Charlie, we could do this all night every night," he whispered softly to the child.

Michelle chuckled when she told the others how Charlie didn't want to leave Alan's arms.

"Why is that funny?" Chasidy asked.

Barlow knew exactly why it was so funny. "AJ all ov'r again," he said laughing also.

12

EMBEDDED SPIRIT

The next morning Mrs. Peterson took it upon herself to run breakfast duty. She was practically finished when Chasidy entered the kitchen. "Good mornan', Mrs. Peterson. You cooked?" Chasidy asked smiling.

"Yes and it felt great!"

"Thank you," Chasidy said. "Feel free to feel great any time you have a mind to."

They shared a giggle. But then Mrs. Peterson spoke seriously. "Thank you for makin' me feel at home h're. You let me decorate yor house. Allowed me free reign in yor kitchen. You made it so easy for me to help my family. You don't know how much that meant ta me.

And then you invite Jeffrey, after da way he carried on, she said in a slightly raised tone."

"Good morning, ladies. I hope I'm not intruding," Mrs. Marshall interrupted, "but I'd like to thank you too. We've only missed one Christmas with Alan. That's when you were in da hospital. He wasn't wandering that far away from Robert when he needed him near 'im. We're glad this didn't have to be da second one."

Chasidy was reminded. "Yeah, da kid'nappan' ruined a lotta holidays. Family should be t'geth'r on Christmas." Y'all have made this Christmas one that will neva be forgotten for two people who mean da absolute world ta me. I'm just glad it turned out so well for all of you." She was happy that Michelle and Alan had their parents with them. But she still wanted to hear how the Marshalls earned their title. "I'm still curious though. Tell me how you b'came temporary."

"Un unk. Look at you tryin' ta cheat," Michelle said walking in with Alan and the rest of the gang.

"I was not," Chasidy defended. "Nobody else was up. It's not our fault y'all are sleep heads. We w're just killan' time." She gave her husband a good morning kiss.

"Sit down everyone. Breakfast is ready," Mrs. Peterson said.

"Can I help with something?" Mrs. Marshall asked.

"Absolutely. Just grab somethin'. It all goes on da table. We should get started b'fore babies start wakin' up."

The talk of catching up consumed the entire breakfast. Barlow explained about the Marshalls. "When Alan ran away from the children's home, he stayed with Mr. and Mrs. Marshall for two years. Then he met me and left them to stay under a railroad track so he could be close to me."

"Are you serious?" Chasidy asked completely shocked. Then she turned her attention to Al. "So, this is the story that was too long to tell. Rob shortened it up pretty good."

"We were devastated to see him leave," Mrs. Marshall added.

"Yeah, but there was no talking him out of it." Mr. Marshall continued. "He just had to get back to Robert. But if we had known he would be living outdoors, we would've tied 'im to the bedpost."

"When we finally met Robert later that year on Christmas Day, we immediately saw the special relationship they shared. Robert delivered firewood to the entire community all by himself so that Alan could spend the day with us."

"A 'sacrifice for a sacrifice' he called it," Mr. Marshall added.

"That's the most unusual love story I've ev'r heard," Mrs. Peterson said. "But absolutely beautiful."

"And you guys are still in love taday," Mr. Peterson said chuckling.

"I wouldn't take a plate full of gold for 'im," Barlow confessed.

"What he said," Al agreed.

"Okay. Y'all bout ta make me cry," Chasidy said. "We need to move on to da next story."

Everyone was wiping their eyes pretending they were not crying. "Yes, let's hear about the babies," Mrs. Marshall said.

Michelle was about to start. "Oh, can I please tell this one?" her mom asked.

"Go for it," Mic agreed.

"Our beautiful new grandbabies w're in da accident with them. Their mom was driving da car that hit them. Da mom sadly died and da babies w're left all alone. No next of kin. Well, when Alan heard that they were orphans, he wasn't having it. He refused to let them grow up alone. And Michy agreed with 'im. Robert and Chasidy thought it be a wonderful idea to present them with da babies as a surprise on Christmas. They thought they w'ren't getting' 'em until taday. They've been h're da whole time with Sam in his bungalow."

The Marshalls and Mr. Peterson were speechless. "That so does not surprise me." Mrs. Marshall said. "Alan left the children's home to find his family. Knowing that those children didn't have a family never would've set well with him."

After hearing the story about Alan, Mrs. Peterson remembered the Marshalls from Amory. "Since we're all family, why don't we lose da formalities. I think first name basis is more than appropriate. Agreed?"

"Agreed." They all said.

None wanted that morning to end. Even when the babies started awakening, they simply joined them at the table. There were plenty of arms to accommodate them. And since everybody wanted their fair share of time with each one, they played the pass-the-baby game while they reminisced of old times, shared new times and touched on hopes of future times. The gang was complete when AJ arrived late at the table after sleeping in.

Even though the accident left him in the darkness unable to see for weeks; Alan had begun to see more clearly than he had ever seen before. He remembered the trying ordeals Rob went through during the past two years. And now his own accident has become an eye opener. Life is precious and time is a precious commodity of it.

As he watched his family over the next few days, he vowed even more to be more intentional in his actions towards his loved ones. He and Michelle were already scheduled to renew their vows in May. But that was months away. He wanted to celebrate his entire family. He and Rob had given their lives to the Lord. In a few weeks they would be baptized. *'A new beginning,'* he thought to himself. Rob will have started his studies of becoming a preacher under Pastor Bishop's mentorship. That's not something he's not going to want to depart from once he's started. However, he had already begun to put in place plans to celebrate his wife, his family, and his life. He was more determined now than ever before to make that happen. Rob had to be a part of that, or it just wouldn't mean the same. He sent AJ home to get a notebook from his desk. Now that everyone was here with him, he wanted to share his plans.

Michelle saw AJ heading for the door. "Where're you goin AJ?"

"Ta get somethin' for Dad from da house."

"By yorself?" Michelle asked looking cross-eyed at Alan.

"He'll be fine, Mic," Al said.

"I'll go with 'im," Mr. Peterson said. "I could use da exercise."

"I'll go too if ya don't mind," Papa Stan said also. "I'd like to see the house."

While they waited for them to return, Alan shared his thoughts. "Y'all know, Mic and I are r'newing our vows in May. I'll let her tell ya about da plans for da weddin'. But I've decided to do somethin' extra special. Somethin' ta celebrate my family," he began. He had everyone's curiosity piqued. "I'm thinkin' about a pre-weddin' party."

"Ugh, AL," Chasidy started, 'FYI, that's nothang' special. Exactly."

AJ and his grandpas were gone every bit of five minutes. Just then he walked in and handed him the notebook. "Here you go, Dad."

"Thanks, Little Guy." Then he said to Chasidy, "It is da way we're doing it. I've chartered a private cruise ship ta sail da to three different countries with our family and friends for da thirty days leading up to da weddin'. I want everyone to join us," he said.

"By everyone, you mean…" Mama Kelly started for clarification.

"My family. All of my family." Then he looked at Chasidy. "That includes *the gang* Chasidy."

"Are you serious?" Chasidy asked excitedly.

"I made a list, but I haven't decided on da destinations yet. Maybe we can do that t'gether. Mic has decided where she wants to get married though. So, they should probably be in near proximity."

That brought an instant smile to her face. "Yeah, we're getting' married in Aruba at Da Ritz-Carlton. I know it's probably childish, but I'm havin' my dream weddin'. A real-life Cinderella Weddin'. You only live once right? My gown will spread from one side of da aisle to da oth'r. There'll hardly be room for Dad ta walk b'side me," she giggled.

Rob looked a definite look at Alan with the most satisfying grin on his face. But Chasidy spoke the words that he had to be thinking. "It doesn't get any dreamier than that when it comes to dream wedd'ans. Count me in."

"You don't have a choice, Girl," Michelle informed her, "Yur my Maid of Honor."

"That's what I'm talkin' about," Chasidy answered, using Michelle's favorite saying.

Alan was sure Rob's smile meant he was on board, especially since Chasidy didn't have a choice. He waited for everyone else's answer. He looked first at the Petersons. Before Mrs. Peterson could speak, Mr. Peterson said, "Son, that's an awful lotta fuss and money to spend on a woman yur already married to."

"Jeffrey!" Mrs. Peterson yelled. "Don't make me put you out again."

Mr. Peterson continued, ignoring his wife. "I'm not even all that big on cruisin' either." Everybody just knew that the newly reformed Mr. Peterson had now become un-reformed. The smile Michelle only moments ago had on her face was now gone. Mr. Peterson who was smiling looked at her and continued, "But there isn't enough water in da ocean ta keep me from walkin' you down da aisle this time." Everyone was relieved that he had learned how to kid around.

Then Al looked at his temporary parents. They answered the question he silently asked. "We didn't miss the first one and we wouldn't miss this one either for anything in the world." Mama Kelly said.

Directing his attention back at Chasidy, "Okay Chasidy. Tell everybody not to use any more vacation time until April," he teased.

"Don't even worry 'bout it. If they get fired, they can all come work fa you," she teased back.

But Rob added, "You got that right!" Rather seriously.

AJ sat holding his little brother, listening to the adults. As he played with Charlie, he thought about the nice nurse who watched over him at the hospital. "Mom. Dad. Can we invite Nurse Tammy on da cruise also? I'll bet she'd like that," he asked.

"Ya know, I was just telling Rob we need to do somethin' special for her for takin' such good care of you." Alan replied.

But it was Mic who said, "We absolutely can invite 'er. But maybe we can do somethin' special for 'er sooner than that. You help us think of somethin', okay."

"So whatta the plans for the honeymoon?" Mama Kelly asked. "Who will watch the children? Stan and I would be glad to keep 'em for ya."

Everyone looked in their direction. Quite naturally, the Petersons assumed that AJ would be with them. But that was before their family miraculously grew two figures. "Of corse, we'll have AJ." Mrs. Peterson said.

Suddenly Alan and Michelle realized that AJ had a whole multiple-choice list of grandparents now. And they had a whole new decision to make. But AJ had adopted his Uncle Rob's responsible fixation towards his little brother. He quickly asked, "What about Charlie?"

"We could take da babies," Mama Kelly answered.

"Yeah, we wouldn't mind that at all," her husband agreed.

"No." AJ protested. "They have to stay with me. Charlie might be scared."

His parents weren't the least bit surprised at that answer. "We agree," Alan said. Mic and I think they should stay t'gether too."

The Marshalls were disappointed. The Petersons felt bad for them. They had just been invited into their grandson's life. They weren't ready to give him up just yet. The Marshalls have had him all of his life. They wanted to play catch up. But Michelle had already decided to ask her parents to stay with AJ at their house. She saw no reason for that to change especially since they had plenty of room for the Marshalls as well. She suggested, "Couldn't da four of you stay at our house and keep da kids for us, t'gether?"

That was Alan's exact thought. "We're b'comin' more and more like Rob and Chasidy each day," he said. "That's exactly what I was thinkin'."

"Hey. We w're soulmates first," Mic corrected, giving him a kiss on the cheek.

#

With the baptismal approaching, the New Year was looking more promising than ever. Especially after Rob shared a bit of information with him about his nephews. He knew Al would be just as excited to hear it as he is to tell it. He knocked softly on the door. "Come in," Al answered.

"How're ya doin?" Barlow asked.

"Great, man."

"Wanna hear somethin' that'll make it bett'r?"

"If that's even possible."

"You decide," Barlow began. "Terrence and Antonio have decided to join us in church t'night. They wanna be there to support us. As far as Terrence is concerned; by us, I mean you." That touched him like nothing else could. Or so he thought.

At the Watch Meet services, they spoke to Pastor Bishop about helping them make a special announcement. After the pastor announced the date for the baptismal and introduced the candidates to the congregation, he asked the young men to the front. "It's a rare thing when a man can have such an influence on a young person that the young person has a desire to learn from that man. It's even rarer if there are two such men." He asked the young men to stand and join Barlow in front of the church. "Stand right here b'side yor father," he said to Terrence and Antonio. Al was sitting on the first pew in front of them. "Sister Chasidy has expressed to me many times how she wished she could get her family in church with her. I can't tell you how it makes me feel to see her family in church tonight. Sister Chasidy, yor sons have something to say."

Antonio spoke first. "Mom, you've been invitin' me and Cait ta church for a long time. So, we decided tonight that w're gonna join church with Dad, Uncle Al, and da rest of da family." Chasidy was elated.

It took Terrence a few minutes to begin. He looked at Alan sitting on the pew for more than a minute or two. He stepped over to shake Al's hand. But that wasn't enough. He extended him a hug also. He had really developed a special kind of love for Alan. Then he turned to Rob still holding Al's hand. He seemed to be stuck as to where to start. When he did start, he said, "I've nev'r met a man I admire and r'spect as much as I do da two of you. You guys are da coolest. I'd follow both of you anywhere cause I know you wouldn't lead me wrong. I'm gonna get baptized too Dad. And learn what you wanna teach about God." With that said, Alan couldn't resist standing to join them in a group hug. Chasidy, Mic, and the rest of the family thought that was splendid idea.

#

Before going to bed that morning after Watch Meet Service, Mr. Peterson had a ton of emotions tumbling around in his heart. They first started with Barlow. He had been so wrong in the comments he made about him. And even more wrong for hating him for no apparent reason. Mrs. Peterson was glad to hear that he no longer felt that way. But she gleamed inside at what she heard next. "My son-in-law is amazin'. His strong love for family emanates all around him. It can be felt by anyone near him. That's why my daughter fell in love with 'im. That's why little Charles didn't wanna leave 'im. That's also why that young man, his nephew, has taken such a liking to 'im. AJ has that same embedded spirit for family love. I was such a fool ta keep them apart for all those years. And da two of you. She couldn't have picked a bett'r young man if he lived in a fancy mansion than da one she pulled out from und'r that railroad track."

Mrs. Peterson agreed with everything her husband had just said except for one thing, "Our daughter," she corrected.

#

\#

As happy as Barlow was for Alan, the secret between him and Michelle troubled him. He had never kept a secret from Alan before. He didn't like doing it now. He didn't care to start the New Year out hiding things. He wasn't sure what to do. If he tells Al, he would be betraying Michelle. If he didn't tell him, he would be betraying his best friend. Something he has never done before. But the most important thing is what it would mean to his ministry. He didn't want to start his work with God with a secret hanging over his head. It would be just honoring a lie.

Chasidy could tell he was troubled about something. He tried to deny it when she asked him about it. But Chasidy is the one person he told himself he would never lie to. "Mic told me somethin' about her father. Somethin' that she has been keepin' from Al for a long time. She doesn't want 'im to know."

"Rob, you've never kept anythang from 'im before, have you?"

"No. Nothin'. And this could ruin all da progress that's been made h're this holiday season. Al's happiness means everythin' to me."

"Maybe you should let Mic know how you feel."

He called Mic into the den where they could have some privacy. "I don't like keeping secrets from Al," he started. "Maybe you should 'im."

"And ruin our relationship. Alan is happier than I've ever seen him. I can't ruin that for him. For us." Mrs. Marshall was walking past the door when she heard them talking. She ear hustled on their conversation.

"Mic. I don't know how long I can keep this from 'im. I don't wanna go into my ministry holding on to this secret. You should be da one to tell 'im. But if you can't, I will." Someone else was coming so Mrs. Marshall walked away before hearing the entire conversation. She rushed to tell Mr. Marshall what she had heard.

Michelle was torn. "Rob, my dad has apologized for his actions towards Al. Maybe we should leave it at that. He sounded really sincere."

"But what if he isn't. Don't you think Al should be aware of that, just in case."

Michelle thought about what Barlow said. He has never stirred her wrong before. "Maybe yur right. It should be Al's decision whether to trust 'im or not. He can't make that decision unless he knows everythin'."

#

The doctors' appointments were scheduled for the same day. Mic and AJ saw the same doctor. He poked and prodded and gave them a thorough looking over. He finally concluded that they were as good as new and released their bandages. Being a fan of old wise tales, he warned that they might be able to predict the weather from now on because of their injuries. Once he explained to AJ what he meant by that; his boyish imagination received it with anticipation, blatantly evident in his response, "That's what's up!" while nodding his little head. Mic, however, could think of better things to look forward to. Like her husband's neck brace coming off. Soon she would know if she anticipated in vain.

Alan was filled with his own anticipation. He didn't feel any more pain. And his neck was no longer swollen. He felt healed. He believed he was healed and so, expected to leave the doctor's office unattached to a neck brace.

It was Al's first-time meeting Dr. Spencer. He was a short stubby guy who looked like he should be a cartoon character. For reasons only known to Al, he felt even more hopeful when he met the animated little man. It's befitting only to Al to find a reason to hope in a cartoon character. Dr. Spencer asked him a rash of questions before carefully removing the brace. Then he asked Al to slowly move his head from side to side and up and down. Al performed like a rock star. Then he checked his eyes to make sure they were functioning properly. When the doctor finished examining Al, he asked him, "Now what was it you came to see me for young man?" Mic didn't think that was funny at all. She was ready to take Al to see somebody else. Anybody else. But Al let out a glorious laugh from deep down in his gut. That was apparently what the humorous little cartoon looking doctor was hoping for. He wanted to make sure Al wasn't in any pain when he laughed. He gladly said to him, "Young man, yur all healed." Now Alan was ready for whatever life threw at him next. That curve ball hit him in the face shortly after they returned home.

He went looking for his parents to share the good news. They were discussing the conversation Mrs. Marshall overheard a few days ago. "I refuse to b'lieve it." Mr. Marshall said. "You must've heard something else."

"I wish I had, Stan. But I know what I heard. We have to tell Alan."

"No. I won't be a part of that."

"If it were you, wouldn't you wanna know that yor wife had an affair with yor best friend?"

Alan swung the door open. "What did you say?"

"Alan!"

"Mama Kel, why would you say something like that? Why would you lie on Mic and Rob?"

"I'm not lying son. I heard them talking about it the other day. I'm so sorry Alan." Alan left without sharing his good news. He wasn't even sure if they noticed his brace was gone.

#

For the next few days, he was in a quiet daze. He barely touched his wife and couldn't stand the sight of Barlow. They both noticed the change in his demeanor. Everyone did. Barlow tried to talk to him about it but made excuses not to.

Alan found the information Chasidy gave him about his past to be more than interesting. He and Michelle continued the research into his childhood with their own private investigator. They were all in the family room having an unusual discussion with Chasidy and AJ about Rob's deceased mom who had visited him just a few months earlier during Chasidy's pregnancy. Barlow had a difficult time believing it. "Chasidy," Barlow said. "Dead people don't walk da earth."

"No, they don't," Chasidy agreed. "But sometimes their spirit returns for a purpose."

"But why do you think it was my mom? If anyone, it was Ethel's spirit in Berta. Even AJ said..."

"I nev'r said she was Grandma Ethel." He interrupted.

Everyone else was looking at the two of them sideways, wondering who they should call for help. All of that changed when a knock came at the door. And they realized that was just the beginning of strange things.

Barlow handed Alan the envelope he was given by the carrier. When Alan opened it and read what was in it; he couldn't believe what he was reading. And he knew no one else would either. "It's a good thang I've got this in writin' or y'all would think I'm as crazy as we think AJ and Chasidy are right now."

"What is it Al?" Michelle asked. He almost didn't answer.

"Rob is my broth'r," he finally said without any excitement at all, looking around the room to see everyone's faces.

"We know, Al," Mic said, referring to their close relationship. "But what does da paper say?"

Alan was paused again. "That is what da paper says." Now, everyone stared at him, like deer stopped in headlights. He mentally slapped himself across the face to bring himself back to Sanityville. Then, he began reading. *"...The parents of da infant that w're killed in da accident w're named James and Patricia Barlow. Alan and Jade Ferguson adopted da infant legally giving him their name along with da father's namesake. James Barlow was previously married ta Roberta Louise Barlow but left her and her son for a Caucasian woman whom he lat'r married. It was da child from that union that was rescued from da accident and adopted by da Fergusons. Young Ferguson ran away from da Chiricahua Children's home where he resided and was nev'r recovered by da state."* When Alan first started reading, tears formed in his eyes. By the time he had finished, he was in full tear flowing mode. No one said a word. Even Rob was speechless.

The Marshalls remembered the day Alan left them to be with Rob, *'a boy about his age.'* They fully understand now that Alan literally had no choice but to leave. He must have prayed an earnest prayer to God from his innocent childish heart for his family. A prayer that God wouldn't allow anything to keep Him from answering. Not even the sincere love of *temporary parents.* "We could never understand why you left us that day. We were so hurt. But months later, when you brought Robert by to meet us, we were comforted, and we knew you were where you were supposed to be."

They thought he had become overwhelmed with joy, but Alan's tears had a different meaning. He became angry when he thought of his wife betraying him with his best friend, now his brother. He dropped the paper on the floor and left the room. Before he left the room, he looked at Barlow and said, "Just one more secret between friends. Right Rob."

He stepped out onto the porch into the fresh air to regain his composure. Mic stood to go after him. "Mic," Chasidy said. "I'm sorry. But it's not you he needs this time, Girl."

"But..." Michelle began to reply. She wasn't so sure after hearing Alan's comment. Was he referring to her and Barlow's conversation? If so, how did he know?

"Rob knows what he has to do," Chasidy coached. Michelle looked at Rob as if asking *whatta you waiting for?'*

Rob took a deep sigh, smiled at Michelle, and went out to the porch to see about his brother. Alan began talking as soon as Rob walked up beside him. "It all makes sense now. Everything." Rob nodded in agreement.

"We w're like two magnets drawn to each oth'r. We still are," Rob added.

"Do you think Ethel knew?" he asked.

"I don't know. I think she would've told us if she did."

"Maybe she did," Alan said. "R'member da last thang she said to us right b'fore she left us? She said it ta both of us."

"Take care of yor broth'r," Rob spoke. "Maybe that's why she fought so hard to win yor love. So, she could keep us togeth'r."

"Does this change anythang b'tween us?" Alan asked him.

"Why would it?"

"My mom broke up yor mom's marriage."

"Our dad broke up my mom's marriage." Barlow corrected him. "Al, I've seen women practically throw themselves under you. You were so in love with Mic, you nev'r turned 'em a look. Our dad had that same option."

"Is that why you slept with Mic?"

"What?" Barlow was stunned.

"Did you know? Is that why you had an affair with my wife? To get back at him through me." Alan repeated himself.

"That's silly Al. Where's this comin' from?"

"Mama Kel heard da two of you talkin' about a secret you couldn't take into yor ministry."

"Alan, she's mistaken. If you weren't so upset, I wouldn't even entertain that with an answer. We weren't talkin' about an affair."

"Then what were you talkin' about?" At that moment Barlow realized what Michelle meant. How sometimes it's best to leave well enough alone. But the seal has been broken. He needed to hear the rest of the story. He needed to hear it from his wife. But since it was his idea to tell him. "Al. Mic told me somethin' at the hospital in confidence while you w're havin' yor x-ray done. Mrs. Marshall overheard me tryin' to convince her to share it with you." He shared it with him instead and hoped it was for the good, "She's afraid it might ruin yor new relationship with her dad. But I thought you should know. I didn't like keepin' a secret from you."

"Then... y'all didn't have an affair?"

"I could nev'r do that to you, and neith'r could Mic. She loves you with every ounce of her being. And so do I. Holdin' a gun to our heads couldn't make us betray you."

Alan was embarrassed that he had even entertained that thought. He felt exactly the same way about them. He had to ask the question again. "So, nothing's changed between us, even aft'r this?" Al needed to hear Rob say they were okay. Especially now.

"I didn't say that. Everythin's changed. It's all for da bett'r. Da man I've called my broth'r for all of our days t'geth'r, really is my broth'r. With da way I feel about you, I can't even be mad at our dad about that. Yur da best gift he could've given me."

Alan thought about what Chasidy and AJ said about Rob's mom. "Maybe that's why Berta, yor mom, took to AJ so. She wanted us to know that she's okay with us being broth'rs. That she forgives our father."

"I didn't know my mom. But I'd like to think that would be exactly somethin' she would do." Barlow replied.

Alan had given Rob a good friend pat on the back for all of their lives. But this was the first time he had given his brother one. "Man, its cold out h're. You could at least invite ya broth'r in outta da chill." They both laughed as they reentered the house.

Michelle and Chasidy were relieved to hear the laughter. "You okay, Baby?" she asked Alan.

"Bett'r than okay," Alan answered. "I'm thinkin' about askin' my broth'r ta be my best man at our weddin'." He seriously joked.

"I feel confident his broth'r will agree to that," Barlow added. "They've got a lotta catchin' up da do."

Then Alan put Michelle's mind at ease and his mother's. "Mic, Rob told me about yor talk. We're good Baby. All of us." Michelle nodded once at Barlow.

Before they could get too settled, AJ had returned from disappearing right after his dad went out on the porch. He handed Chasidy a book.

Upon first look, she recognized the journal. "This is Ethel's. Where'd you get it?"

"From Grandma Berta," AJ answered. "She said to give it to you, and you would know what to do with it."

She opened the journal and it fell open to a certain page. Her eyes grew big as she began to read. She didn't give a forewarning before she read out loud. *"My friend visited me in a dream last night with an unusual request. "First of all," she said, "thank you for taking such good care of my boy. He's so handsome and he's coming along splendidly. A fine young man he'll be. But I need you to do something for me," she said.*

I asked her what else could I do?

She said, "Robert doesn't mix well with other children. He spends much too much time alone. Which is why his brother will soon find him. I need you to take care of him for me. Robert needs his brother, and his brother needs him."

I asked her how I would know his brother. She said "You don't need to know him because they will know each other. They won't understand why but they will be instantly drawn to each other. You must keep them together, Ethel. It won't be easy. The boy has trust issues. But his desire to stay with his brother will outweigh that. They need each other. And they need you." I awakened from my dream a nervous wreck.

The silence in the room was as thick as smoke. No one knew what to say. But then Rob remembered the question Al asked out on the porch a few moments ago. "I guess that answered yor question about Ethel."

He chuckled just a little thinking on his amazing God. "God left no questions unanswered. He wanted it to be clear that He made all of these miracles possible. From the time we first met." Al concluded.

The atmosphere in the room was much too solemn for Chasidy. Her thought process went into overdrive once again trying to liven things up. "So, after all that, Al, you still have an identity crisis," she started.

"Why do ya say that?" Alan asked her.

"B'cause, knowan' what we know now, that would really make you Alan Jr, not Sr."

Alan pretended to ponder. "Ya know, yur right. And that would really make 3rd Al, 'Not' 3rd Al," he reasoned with his Chester cat grin.

"Al, I'm not callan' my baby is 'Not 3rd Al'."

"What about 3rd Al 2?" he suggested.

"That'll work," Chasidy agreed. They all shared a laugh.

13

FAMILY IS EVERYTHING

It was difficult for Alan to get to sleep that night. His adrenaline was working overtime. Mic physically felt her husband's joy. But like other times, she felt him wrestling with something. "What is it. Al? What's on yor mind?" she asked.

He smiled at her approvingly. "I love it when you do that. Yur so in tune ta me," he said. "I was just thankin' about maybe workin' parttime so that I can spend more time with you and da kids."

Michelle proudly reminded him, "Al. You own half da company. You don't have to work at all if you don't want to."

Alan laughed a joyous laugh. "Yur absolutely right," he said, "thanks to my broth'r."

"You've said da word 'broth'r' exactly sixty-two times since you found out Rob is blood related to you. I get it. Yur happy," she teased. But then said sincerely. "And I couldn't be happier for ya." Then she caressed his neck where the brace used to be. "Is that why we're still here with them? B'cause you can't bear to leave 'im?"

"This Holiday has been one I could have nev'r imagined," he began. "And no, I don't want it to end. So, I guess that would be a 'yes' in a way." He finally concluded.

"But, my overly sentimental husband, if the holiday doesn't end then our life stops here. As good as this is, I'm lookin' forward to my Cinderella Weddin' with my Prince Charming," she reminded him of the future they had to look forward to.

"Yur so right again." But he was determined to keep his family together. All of his family. He said to Mic, "When we go back home, our parents might go home too."

"Yes, probably." Mic agreed.

"I'm not ready for them to go yet. Are you?"

"No. But whatta you thinkin'?"

"Why don't we ask them to stay. I know AJ would love it. And they could have an active part in their grandchildren's lives."

"I like that idea. But I'm sure they don't wanna be shacked up with us for da rest of their lives." Mic reasoned.

"No. Just long enough for their own homes to be built. We have enough land. I can take care of everything," Al explained.

"Yeah, thanks to my sister," she teased.

"And my broth'r," he teased back. They both laughed. "Do you think they'll go for it?"

"We won't know unless we ask."

The next morning, AJ was up bright and early to do stable duty. Al asked him to wait until after breakfast. AJ was anxious to see his horse. "Dad, Silver's gonna wonder where I am," AJ complained.

"Silver will be just fine for another thirty minutes," his dad said.

Breakfast was rather quiet, except for small talk every once in a while. Rob sensed something in the making with Al and Mic. He wondered what was going on with them. Chasidy had begun her own thought process as well. Chasidy's country girl mannerism wouldn't let her linger in wonder for long. She finally blurted out. "Okay, girl. What's going on? Y'all fixin' ta leave us?" Everybody stopped eating. Rob looked specifically at Al. Al took his time looking at everyone at the table.

"Are you done with yor breakfast, Little Guy?" he asked AJ.

"Yes," AJ answered.

"Is everyone else done?" he asked his family.

"Yes," they each replied.

"Chasidy let's take da babies for a walk," Mic suggested. Chasidy looked at Rob and he at her.

"Okay," Chasidy agreed out of curiosity.

"Let's all go for a walk," Al added, "while AJ tend to da horses."

"I'll help ya get da quad ready," Barlow told Chasidy.

"I think b'tween four grown women, da group of us is capable of gettin' six babies ready for a walk." Mic said. "You stay with yor broth'r." They both grinned.

They enjoyed the leisurely walk through The Grove listening to the story Al told of how they came to live so close to each other. He pointed out where the one property ended and the other began. Barlow and Chasidy listened attentively. They walked behind the house to the stables where AJ was already embracing

Silver. "Well, this certainly is a nice place y'all have here," Papa Stan said. "The house is just as beautiful on the inside," he told his wife.

Al and Mic glanced a definite look at each other. By now, they all knew the two of them had something on their minds. "AJ. Come over here for just a second," his dad called. "Chasidy, Mic never answered yor question from earlier. We are ready to come home." He paused again. "We're not ready for this to end though."

"Whatta you mean, Son?" Papa Stan asked.

"Mic and I were wonderin' if y'all might wanna live a little closer to yur grands. I'm sure AJ would like that."

"Like it! Dad, I would love it!" AJ said excitedly.

"As you can see, we have a nice stretch of land out here. We could build you places of ya own. You'd still have ya privacy. AJ and his brother and sister would have their grandparents near. And Mic and I would have our family near us."

"Let's get da babies outta da cold, go inside and talk about it," Mic suggested. It wasn't a decision that involved Rob and Chasidy. They concluded they were only there for moral support. So, they refrained from voicing an opinion either way. When Mama Kelly saw the inside of the house, she was completely taken aback. The elegantly designed ranch house from the outside suggested the same ambience once inside. But instead, the rooms were warm, cozy, and just the right size for family gatherings.

After a formal tour of the place, they nestled in the family room to make a final decision. "Well, Al said, "Whatta you thinkin'?" Both sets of grandparents were bursting to speak. But neither of them wanted to show how anxious they were. So, Al started with his parents. "Mom. Pop, is this something you would consider doin'?"

"Kelly, whatta you think?" Papa Stan asked.

"Al are saying that you would build us our own place out here on this beautiful property so that we can be near you, Mic and our grandchildren?" his mom asked.

"Yes, mam," he answered gladly.

"How can I say no to that?" she answered with another question.

"Just what I wanted to hear!" Al said.

"Mom. Dad." Mic coached her parents.

Mrs. Peterson knew what her answer would be. But she purposely encouraged her husband to answer. She knew that with their history his answer would mean more to Michelle and Alan. "Go ahead, Jeffrey. Tell them what's on yor mind."

It took him a moment or two to get started. He just sat there shaking his head in disbelief. Barlow thought he would help him out a little. "Mr. Peterson, forgiveness is da key to healin'. That includes forgivin' ya'self too."

Al and Mic walked over to sit beside Mr. Peterson. They each put their arms around him. AJ joined them, stopping in front of him and kneeling between his knees. "Grandpa, please stay. You can help me take care-a Silver and da others. And we can go ridin' t'geth'r. All of us."

"Yeah, Mr. Peterson," Chasidy added. "Somebody needs to keep my paisley beauty active until I can ride."

"Dad, whatta you say?" Mic asked one last time.

Mr. Peterson took a deep breath. "After all da horrible things I did ta you two. Keepin' you apart. Keepin' you and yor mom apart. Sayin' those awful things to ya." He looked directly at Michelle. "Breakin' yor heart." Then back at Alan. "You would still build me a house so that I could be near my grandchildren? What kind of a man are you?"

"Nothin' special, Sir. Just one who loves his family. Family is everythin' ta me." Alan humbly replied.

"I beg to differ, Son. I beg to differ. You are special indeed."

#

Barlow and Chasidy were enjoying having a full house. They suggested they wait until after the baptism to move back home. Rob especially wasn't ready to let go of Al just yet. They both were talking themselves into the separation process.

The following Monday Michelle was scheduled for a visit with her Cardiologist. She soon learned that the Christmas Miracle season is still in full bloom well over into the month of January. Her doctor ran his usual tests. However, being baffled by the results, he sent her down to have some x-rays done as well. That bothered Alan. "Is somethin' wrong, Doc?"

"That's what I'm hoping the x-ray will tell us," The Doctor answered. He could see the worry in their faces. "Now you hold all of that until we get done. There's no need for worry unless we have somethin' ta worry ov'r," he advised. When she returned from x-ray, he continued with his questioning. "Are you still regularly takin' yor medications Mrs. Ferguson?"

"Well, I've been kinda slack during da holidays. It got so busy sometimes, we have new babies...I forgot to take it," she said looking at Alan.

"New babies?" the doctor asked.

"Yes, a two-year-old and his newborn sister. Al and I are planning to adopt them," she explained.

The doctor continually looked at the x-ray results.

"What is it, Dr.?" Alan asked again.

"Could be nothing," he said, "could not be."

"What does that mean?" Michelle asked.

"It means either my equipment is broken or yor heart isn't anymore. I can't find a single thing wrong with it," the doctor proclaimed.

Michelle was near speechless. Only able to breathe one word, "What?" She stared back and forth between Al and her doctor with tear trenched eyes.

"It must be those new babies," the doctor said smiling. "They have a special way of fixin' our hearts sometimes.

Alan could see she didn't understand, so he explained it to her. "Anoth'r Christmas Miracle," he said. "I don't know what God's tryin' ta tell us. But He's got my full attention."

#

Mrs. Peterson accompanied Mic to her doctor's appointment. When she told her the news about her heart, it was mind-blowing. They three deemed this news too important to share over the phone. Al let Mic do the sharing. She walked into the family room and modeled a happy pose. "Do you see anythin' different about me?" she asked.

"No," Chasidy replied.

"Me neither," agreed Barlow.

Her dad and the others just stared at her. "I'll bet if my son was here, he could see da difference."

"Girl, are you gonna tell us or do I have to go snatch 'im outta school?" Chasidy protested.

"My heart is healed!" she said excitedly. She picked up little Grace and kissed her on her cheek. "Now I don't have to be worried about takin' care of you and Charles." Chasidy and Barlow couldn't think of a better way to end the holiday season. He gave a definite look to Al and nodded once. Al donned his Chester cat grin.

The Marshalls were elated for them. And her mother felt every bit of joy she was feeling inside. But it was Mr. Peterson who felt the greatest joy. His daughter was healed from the pain that he had caused her. He knew now that she had truly forgiven him.

After the baptismal, Barlow helped Al move his family home. When they were done, they hugged like they were never going to see each other again. When they finally let go of each other, they had a brief heart-to- heart.

"Old habits are hard to break, I guess," Rob said.

"What's that mean?" Al asked.

"You would think aft'r thirty-nine years, I'd be well past tryin' ta watch ov'r you. Takin' care-a you was embedded in my spirit from when I first saw ya. I guess yur old enough to take care-a ya'self now."

"No way, Buddy," Al said. "We made a promise to Ma Ethel ta nev'r stop takin' care of each oth'r. No weaselin' out on me."

"I'm happy for you Al. Enjoy ya family."

"Don't be talkin' like this is good-bye. We live fifteen seconds away from each oth'r." They shared a laugh. "And we have two houses ta build, so we're gonna get plenty of bro-time t'geth'r."

"Bet," Barlow said. Then headed home.

#

He walked through the door and met Chasidy's smile waiting for him. "Hi beautiful."

"Hi yorself, handsome." Chasidy hadn't seen her husband this sad; aside from Ethel's death, since before they built the New Little House. She knew exactly what was wrong with him. "Yur not losan' 'im, Rob," she told him.

"It sure feels like it," he answered, not even trying to deny his concerns.

"There'll be a hard freeze in hell b'fore Al let that hap'an." She consoled him.

Just then his phone rang. "It's Al," he told Chasidy smiling. "What is it, Buddy? Didn't I just leave you?"

"What? A fella can't miss his broth'r?" Rob laughed. "Naw, I just wanted you to know, yur not losin' me. In fact, now that I'm retired like my broth'r, yur gonna get tired of lookin' in my face."

"That'll nev'r hap'en Al," he promised. "Nev'r."

Barlow was on board with the idea of Alan spending more time with his family. They both agreed Bradley and Gabe should be made co-executives of the company and Gonzalez a main lead in the field. Everything else was already a well- oiled machine.

Alan began construction on the bungalows in February. It reminded Barlow of the time he met Chasidy. It reminded Al of the same thing; only how much he missed Barlow during his getting acquainted time with Chasidy. "I'll bet I know what yur thankin' about?" Al said to him one day while they were working.

"Take yor best shot," Barlow said.

"Chasidy."

Rob chuckled. "Yeah. When we w're buildin' da Litte House," he said.

Al grinned at Rob. He had read his mind perfectly. But he said something different instead, "Oh. I thought you w're thankin' about her being okay with us runnin' off fishin' every oth'r weekend. I thank it's time to start that ball rollin'. Let's knock off and go give da boat a test run."

"What about AJ and ya dads?" Rob asked not really wanting to share his bro-time.

"AJ has a new brother and sister, two sets of grandparents, and a beautiful mom ta hold his attention. I've only got one broth'r." It was Al's way of saying he shared his sentiment. "B'sides, if my son's gonna drive a boat; I need to know that it's safe." They shared a chuckle.

Alan texted Mic, "Gone fishing with my brother."

Rob texted Chasidy, "My brother and I are headed to the lake to try out the boat."

Mic replied, "That's what I'm talking about."

Chasidy replied, "Aren't you glad y'all married me?" with a smiley face emoji.

#

Michelle's Cinderella wedding went off like a dream. Alan's pre-wedding cruise put everyone in a romantic mood and got everyone extra hyped for the special occasion. AJ's special guest was Nurse Tammy. She enjoyed escorting him around the cruise ship.

He set sail with his family through the Gulf of Mexico headed towards Panama where they enjoyed the warm beaches of the San Blas Islands. Cait and her grandchildren have always been water babies. So, Chasidy and Rob were on their own with the quad. They offered to keep Grace as well so Al and Mic could enjoy the beaches with their family. From there they sailed to the small islands of Curacao and Bonaire stopping and disembarking for days enjoying the entertainment and culture each island had to offer. They arrived in Aruba one day before the wedding.

Michelle's Cinderella wedding went off like a dream. She felt twenty-five years younger strolling down the aisle towards Alan. She felt as if she was floating on air as her elegant Dolce & Gabbana strapless gown gracefully swayed from side to side. Alan and Michelle didn't recall being this nervous the first time they married. They were so lost in the very pleasure of giving their hearts to each other all over again, that neither of them even remembered saying, "I do."

When Pastor Bishop gave permission for Al to kiss his bride, he reached back to loosen her hair, gently fixed it to the shape of her lovely face and kissed her for what felt like the very first time.

Not imagining anything could be more perfect than their beautiful wedding, their honeymoon proved them wrong. One so perfect, in fact, that Alan posed the question one quiet evening while watching the sunset together, "Why haven't we done this b'fore?"

Michelle was much too eager to answer him. "B'cause my darlin' husband is as much a workaholic as his broth'r."

He pulled the pin from her hair to let it fall and fashioned it to the shape of her lovely face. "No more of that," he promised. "In fact, I'm buying that short rope as soon as we get home."

Michelle smiled. "Are you keepin' up with all these promises yur makin' ta me?"

"I have every single one written in my heart."

"That's what I'm talkin' about," she said proudly.

14

DREAM OR NO DREAM

After arriving home from his honeymoon, Alan couldn't hug his family long enough. The love for family has been embedded into his spirit ever since his birth. It was that spirit that caused him to leave Chiricahua Children's Home when he was only ten years old. It was that spirit that made him leave a loving couple and the comfort of their beautiful home to lodge under a railroad track to be near a boy that he knew nothing about. It was that spirit that made him reconnect with the Marshalls months later when he couldn't seem to erase them out of his heart. But more than any of this, it was that spirit that kept him devoted to his own family, doing all that he possibly could to make certain they were always happy and cared for. Family is everything to Alan. Sometimes this all felt surreal to him.

He and Barlow relaxed until nearly eleven o'clock out on the lake one evening. Chasidy did a good thing giving AJ a boat fully equipped with every piece of fishing gear he would possibly need. Al lingered in a state of unbelievable bliss from all that's happened. "Rob, r'member when we first met as boys?" he asked his brother.

"Yeah," Rob laughed. "You let ol Smokey get da best of ya, fell out of a tree and hit yor head."

"Yeah," he agreed. "So, what if I'm still layin' there knocked out? And all of this is a dream."

Rob started laughing hysterically. "We talked about yor stupid questions, Al. Shut up and fish." The two of them were right where they wanted to be. Together.

When he left the children's home looking for his family, he was imagining finding people who looked like him. The Marshalls looked nothing like him. Ethel Middleton looked nothing like him. Whitmer Sanderford and Rebecca Barlow looked nothing like him. But they will forever hold a special place his heart. A place reserved just for family.

Nothing, however, like Robert Barlow who took hold of his heart at the age of thirteen and held it captive for the rest of their lives. The same Robert Barlow who turned out to be his real biological brother. Young Alan Ferguson left the children's home running. He ran full speed into the very family he expected to find; in the very unexpected form of people who looked absolutely nothing like him. For that he is extremely thankful and grateful to God. And forever will be.

Thank you for purchasing Trestle Rat-The Story of Al, the last book in the Barlow Trilogy. I hope you enjoyed it. And I would greatly appreciate it if you would leave a review where you made your purchase so others will know how much you enjoyed it.

But guess what fans! The Family Saga continues with the next generation of Barlows and Fergusons. Visit my website at www.buszyhands.com to find out about new releases and more.

Thanks for your purchase!!!

The Barlow Trilogy

ABOUT THE AUTHOR

D.M. Williams

A Mississippi native who loves to write about the beauty of nature, the southern culture, her home state, faith, God and the wonderful miracles He still performs. Williams writes engaging family saga page-turners filled with spiritual phenomena, humor, relatable issues, love, joy, sadness, and romance from cover to cover. She often voices her discord with issues like bullying, domestic violence, child abuse, and racism cleverly crafted inside her pleasantly entertaining stories. Even though her stories are realistically relatable, as a hopeless romantic, she always finds a place for every girl's fantasy and always a happy-ever-after ending.

Please visit her blog, Buszy Hands Write at Buszyhands.com. Stay in the know, join her fan club and get a FREE SHORT STORY- Clover Valley's Storm.

Email: donnamarie@buszyhands.com.